RURAL ODYSSEY III
Dreams Fulfilled and Back to Abilene

A FICTIONAL AND HISTORICAL NARRATIVE

Mark J. Curran

Order this book online at www.trafford.com
or email orders@trafford.com

Most Trafford titles are also available at major online book retailers.

This is a work of fiction. All of the characters, names, incidents, organizations, and dialogue in
this novel are either the products of the author's imagination or are used fictitiously.

Print information available on the last page.

ISBN: 978-1-6987-0709-9 (sc)
ISBN: 978-1-6987-0708-2 (e)

Trafford rev. 04/28/2021

www.trafford.com
North America & international
toll-free: 844-688-6899 (USA & Canada)
fax: 812 355 4082

THANKS TO THOSE WHO SENT ME IDEAS

PROLOGUE

All right, I'm going to spoil it. This is a "feel good" story. The reader may remember "Rural Odyssey II" from the events of 1966. After that scare in Abilene and subsequent events I have spent this past year in Providence as a Ph.D. student at Brown. Serious girlfriend Mariah Palafox has spent the year as well in Boston at Harvard Law School. There is a lot to tell, but before me and her, an update on my family and situation in Abilene and Mariah's family in Kansas City.

Mom and Dad, Molly and Sean, are doing fine, but now are getting up in years. Aches and pains, more so with Mom with a bad back and osteoporosis and traction in the hospital for the pain. They manage to have a good retirement centered around life at St. Andrew's Catholic Church, Mom in the D of I's, Dad in the Knights of Columbus and a regular pall bearer at funerals (gulp) and carpentry work at church when called upon. He still has the horse barn out at the old farm for town kids boarding their animals, and he still does that huge garden north of the old pond. Mom still gets to her bridge club, and oh, Dad still to his Gin Rummy games down at the Elks Club on Sunday afternoons. We are in touch via the weekly letter (an old custom) and phone calls. My sister Caitlin and husband Ron are doing well on the farm, but with now four kids! Will the Irish – German partnership work out? We'll see. Brother Joe in the Pacific, brother Paul in the Northwest. No rest for the wicked.

Abilene settled down after the Eisenhower Center bombing, the trial and we hope life in prison for the culprits (pardon my skepticism from the past). And that business up in Idaho. Dad and Ron both tell me that farmers are upon hard times, the usual with unknown weather, but spiraling farm machinery prices and low crop prices, many local farmers, including some friends, have sold the farms. Grady Zimmerman and the Clay Wommer family among them. Ron and brother Stan have held on and are doing well because they have a diversified operation – farming and feedlot – and have more land to farm than most of the small operations. Ironically, and I don't understand why, land prices have skyrocketed as well. Why would you want to get into this? Not a good time to buy unless you are a greedy corporation.

In town you see some shuttered storefronts of the old places I grew up with and talked of in "Rural Odyssey II." Old William Donaldson however is still running the "Abilene Reflector Chronicle," and Father Kramden is now pastor and promoted to monsignor at St. Andrew's. Sheriff Wily holds on to that perennial job as sheriff (he will always have the job mainly due to that yeoman work with the bombing incident and capturing the culprits). And Wally Galatin is still at the photo studio and Frank's Friendly Tavern on 3rd Street. More to my / our situation, the Juco has thrived and recently been granted State Department of Education permission to become a four – year college. I'm not surprised. Dean Halderson is a go – getter. Both Mariah and I miss our good days there for those three years as rookie teachers, and the good times with juco colleagues, but more so the students and their families. Old high school buddies have mainly moved on, but Jeremiah Watson still works at the foundry in Enterprise and his Dad still shepherds his flock at the Ebenezer First Gospel Church. What else? I'll fill you in as I get the news.

Mariah's family in Kansas City are much the same, after all it has only been one year. Benjamin and Ariel are doing well, have visited Mariah once in Boston. I took a shuttle in from Providence, and we all had dinner at the famous Oyster House on Faneuil Square. Kansas City news, much the same, Benjamin's practice going well, Ariel doing fine, Mariah's brother Josh the lawyer has become a full partner in his firm specializing in corporate crime. The whole family has a sense of social consciousness, and since there is no lack of crime, Josh and colleagues are busy. The main issues are tax evasion and monopolizing markets. You can imagine, the international sector of the firm is busy – offshore shenanigans, money laundering, and mainly tax evasion.

I had said one year ago that the nation was on to scary times, but Idaho and the extremist people are on the back burner compared to national turmoil and upheaval. There are 190,000 US troops in Vietnam and President Johnson says we will stay until Communism is defeated. I just read that number has jumped to 250,000 and Dr. Martin Luther King just made a speech against the war. On a lighter note, John Lennon of the Beatles said, "We're more popular than Jesus." He recanted later saying he didn't mean to be making "a lousy anti-religious statement."

Here's what has been happening with me and Mariah that first year.

PART I

1

BROWN AND HARVARD

I am well into the graduate studies and the Ph.D. Program in Spanish and Latin American Studies, and things are a whole lot different than back at the undergraduate Jesuit School in Kansas City. This is secular education a la Ivy League. I am getting my first taste of learning Portuguese and love it. Brown has two or three topflight professors teaching the Brazil variant, but I am perhaps not wholly surprised by the emphasis on the continent and Portugal in the department. After all, New England has the Portuguese connection to Lisbon, the many immigrants from that country and all the people coming in from the Azores and Cabo Verde. All the above in conjunction to the New England whaling industry is a given in Providence and along the Rhode Island and Massachusetts coast. There are benefits however, what I might call a two – week "junket" all expenses paid for select Ph.D. students to Lisbon on semester break. It was beautiful but a shock with the language variant. As mentioned, there is the Ivy League atmosphere, a big "Eastern" school population (I think the term is "WASP") and my first exposure to many very intelligent Jewish students. One very happy circumstance would change my life.

Professor Thomas Skidmore is on board after a highly successful stay at the University of Wisconsin, but now "home" for him is Brown in New England. His Latin American Politics and History courses are the absolute best, and especially his emphasis on Brazil and his wonderful book

"Politics in Brazil 1930 – 1964 An Experiment in Democracy," the best such new research available. *This* is one of the main reasons I had chosen Brown (along with proximity to Mariah in Boston). He has the Harvard post – graduate connection and all the prestige to go with it. Better yet, his lectures are informative, enthusiastic and I daresay, entertaining. I never but never miss a lecture, and my hard work and the small classes have led to times out of class for a beer or two and his getting to know the Kansas farm boy as well.

And another course on anthropology used Charles Wagley's seminal "Introduction to Brazil," a phenomenal base for specialized study. In sum, the language, politics, history, and area studies this first year were challenging and rewarding.

There was not much time for fooling around outside of class, but Mariah and I had a good reunion on a weekend later in the Fall when she hopped a bus to Providence, stayed in the graduate girls' dorm and we went around campus, got to a Brazilian restaurant, and had a full day walking tour in Newport. All those seaside old money mansions were a must, like the Vanderbilt's "Breakers;" we just walked by and marveled. I honestly did not know much of that slice of American life, but the Vanderbilt and Rockefeller names were familiar. Incidentally, it was a gorgeous fall day, none better than those in New England with the foliage. Mariah jested, "Oi, ole' goy, you have not mentioned Jewish Heritage and I'm going to one up you – we've got to get to the Touro Synagogue. I hate to spring this on you, but I have been thinking of it ever since you invited me here for the weekend."

We did the walk – by and just popped our heads in the door. It is the oldest in the U.S., 1763, but with the threat of war (the Revolutionary War of 1776-7) its Torah was transferred to the old synagogue in New York. It was founded by her people, Sephardic Jews, so that added an emotional touch to the visit. I've told all about her family's background and how we were with them in "Rural Odyssey II," no need to repeat here. We did the short tour and Mariah was happy.

I said, "Okay, now there's a Catholic place down the way we've got to see, Salve Regina College! Tit for tat. It is run by the Sacred Heart Nuns and there must be some money, an upscale place. And oh, Providence has Providence College. We don't need to see it, but I've got a funny story and I swear it's true. A friend back in Kansas swears when he was there, they brought a live horse up the dorm stairs and put it in a room. Discovered of course and with Dominican discipline the friend and buddies were put on probation, but no dismissal. Just thought you'd like to know even those nasty Dominicans appreciate good blue – blood mares. The nearest Jesuit school is Boston College, maybe we can see that someday."

What a great fun day, so much of U.S. history; we had another fun dinner that night, this time to a Portuguese restaurant and Mariah was back on the shuttle with a lot of study before Monday morning. You may wonder, where do Mariah and I stand? The whole back – east time started when we were very close, intimate at times, no engagement but both her and my parents were wondering. It was a joint decision to think of the future, advanced degrees and then see what would happen. Her dorm accommodation at Brown did not allow much of an update on, uh, that, but we were both "clicking" and planned a real encounter, if you know what I mean, in New York, tourism for both of us.

2

MANHATTAN

That happened in Spring Break now in 1967. Mariah got the shuttle from Boston to Providence and we both got the rickety Providence – New York shuttle bus and experienced my first tour in the metropolis, bunking due to a friend of Mariah's family in a "guest" apartment in upper Manhattan not far from Columbia University. The family uses it for visitors coming into the city and we had it all to ourselves. I think I said that Mariah had been to New York more than once with her parents, in part because of the family's religious connections there. We got to know each other again the first night, still compatible and still I think you could say, "in love." There was no talk, initially, of the future but both of us deciding to have a fun time in the city. Mariah had not exactly had that much time for getting around either, but said she was saving the best places for our visit. I haven't said, but she was as gorgeous as ever, the auburn hair and green eyes and the nicely curved body. I had a full three days away from Brown, so we really got around.

Mariah was familiar with the subway system from former visits, and I've got to say it was a pleasant surprise for the country boy, efficient, some cars shiny new, others beat up and with graffiti in the stations. The C Train had a diverse crowd on board, as expected, a Babel of languages and nationalities. Where to first? The boat tour around the Island. The subway took us to just two blocks from the quay, and then with tourists from all over the country and maybe the world, dressed for the occasion (Mariah warned the air and water in late March could be very cold; I said no more than Providence) we did that "obligatory" introduction to New York.

We both were bundled up with winter coats, stocking caps, gloves, and me in my old insulated, Gore-Tex hiking boots (I think boots are best on New York streets anytime, but these were leather topped with a nice shine and could pass the "ok" test) and Mariah in the equivalent. A good thing, there was a steady if not strong breeze the whole time, and we would only venture outside for the highlights. A glass enclosed seating area with hot chocolate, coffee and sandwiches came in handy. One surprise was when this student colleague from Brown came up, waved at us, all smiles, and said "What a surprise!" He lives out on Long Island, but like everyone else was doing tourism. "If you can believe it, this is my first time on the Grand Circle Tour. Hey, New Yawk ain't half bad. But if you want to see it at its best, it's the borough of Long Island and the places F. Scott Fitzgerald wrote about in 'The Great Gatsby.' But, hey, it's good to be back to civilization huh? Brown is fine but the area sucks." We all laughed, me the Kansas farm boy defending New England – "You can't beat New England for history and beautiful forests and lakes." Highlights of the boat trip, hmm. The Statue of Liberty, the Staten Island Ferry dock on the lower end of Manhattan, the view of Manhattan from the East River, but for me it was the Brooklyn Bridge.

The Brooklyn Bridge

I would have bought that one had anyone offered it. I hadn't been to San Francisco yet and seen the Golden Gate Bridge, but Mariah had and said it's apples and oranges. However, I'm sorry for one big disappointment – the grungy water especially on the East River, a surprise since the ocean comes in there. Someone says it is the bilge from all the huge ocean liners and cargo boats and who knows what else from the city. I don't know. The Hudson was better, but not much; veterans said you should have seen it twenty years ago, it's like the Fountain of Youth now!

Ellis Island

Oh, just for history, the Ellis Island immigration building. Mariah said she remembers the relief expressed by her parents when learning that Ellis Island was closed in 1954, having heard horror stories of that ordeal from older relatives now in the U.S. "Later on, immigration was all handled at the airport or the ship docks, and that was bad enough, but if you had the right papers, and more importantly, the right connections, it was just like a long wait today to get your passport checked and go through your luggage, going through those long lines. Dad and Mom's people came much earlier, the end of the 19ᵗʰ century, first to New York, then to school in Chicago, and then on to Kansas City, and of course Uncle David's people to Mexico City at about the same time."

My turn, I went on to say, "I'm not even sure of any of that with Dad and Mom's families, but I know it was a lot earlier, probably in the 1840s. My parents did not have many details except that Dad's people came from Ireland in the '40s as I said, victims of the era of the Potato Famine, worked in coal mines in eastern Ohio before they got a chance to move to Southeast Nebraska and rented small farms from successful Irish immigrants from a generation before. I can't imagine the hardships, but

Dad and Mom have both told me of pretty rough living conditions in those old clapboard farmhouses."

Mariah said, "I know the general history of my ancestors, the Sephardi (you remember our time in Mexico and Spain two years ago, huh?), and of course no Jewish family is unaware of the pogroms in both Eastern Europe and elsewhere and Hitler's crimes. But Dad and Mom have never gone into great detail; Dad always says, 'Let's just leave well enough alone. It was a horrible time, mostly behind us, so try and be optimistic about the future.' I think I've done that, but no Jewish person I know ever really forgets the past. And Mike, maybe the worst thing: we have learned to not advertise the fact we are Jewish, isn't that as your Mother would say, (I heard her several times) 'a fine kittle of fish?' I can only compare that to the whole Irish 'shtick' of St. Patrick's Day, the Macy Parade, and schmaltzy Bing Crosby songs. Our celebrations and jokes (and you know our people have survived only through humor) are in our homes and 'you know who's coming' to dinner.' Which reminds me, you haven't said anything, do we still have this 'just friends' gig or is there more?"

"If I had thought Ellis Island would have brought this all on, I think I would have suggested the Bronx Zoo instead!" I looked into Mariah's green eyes, planted a kiss on those inviting lips and said, "Let's talk about it tonight. But ole' gal, we have both come a long way! Brown and Harvard Law! I'm off the farm tractor and you're off the perfume counter at that department store in Kansas City (a part – time high school job before K.U. in Lawrence). Oh, did I say, you sure do smell nice! Is that Chanel n. 5? Yuck. Yuck."

The Plaza Hotel, New York

After that chilly ride we hopped an 8th Avenue bus north and got off at Columbia Circle on the southwest edge of Central Park. Jeeze, this is famous. The New York Athletic Club and the Plaza Hotel are just down the street and 5th Avenue beyond. It was already lunch time, so we decided to splurge and "do lunch" in the Plaza. Central Park and other important stuff would be later. Lunch was light after we saw the pricey menu, but soup and a sandwich and coffee sufficed. There was a young lady playing piano in a corner of the huge lobby, and we stopped and listened to her. I couldn't help it, me remembering that three – month music "gig" at the Italian Pizza place, the 5050 Club in Kansas City where I sang folk music and played classic guitar after I graduated from the local Jesuit College. What a deal – the pianist is not a New Yorker but a transplant from Salt Lake! We chatted for a minute or two only, but she admitted she had one of the best of all possible jobs in New York City.

Interior, Plaza Hotel

Mariah and I walked through all the public areas of the Plaza, seeing the original paintings which reminded me of Renoir ("Ha!," Mariah said, "How would you know?") "Intuition my dear, intuition." But maybe more memorable were the large black and white photos of past Plaza guests - The Beatles, Brigitte Bardot, and a vintage photo of Jackie now Onassis and the Greek tycoon and little John Jr. between them. You do get an idea of this place just from that. The chandeliers, paintings and all say, "old money!" Mike and Mariah, you are not in Kansas anymore.

We walked a long way through Central Park, the ponds still half frozen and some skiffs of snow under the trees all the way to the Natural History Museum. The park was pretty, and I guess historic mainly because of its surroundings, one of a kind, but the trees and lakes around Providence and the seaside spectacular scene of Newport seemed as nice. But that Museum and particularly its entrance made a believer out of me!

President Teddy Roosevelt

The statue of President Teddy Roosevelt. In spite of those old photos of him with a rifle and he on his knees and with "granny glasses" beside a huge African elephant with huge tusks, old hunting days, he saw the light and preserved more land in our country than any other president. There is a huge taxidermy look alike elephant in one of the lobbies. The museum for me was a bit emotional because the wonderful nature dioramas brought back one of the most exciting days of my youth when Dad, Mom and I visited Denver, maybe only one of two vacation trips from the farm. We went to the Natural History Museum with its dioramas and little Mike with his machete went slashing through the jungles of Africa and South America!

For Mariah and me though, another salon brought back memories, the Maya and Aztec rooms with stelae, carved altars, and gold and jade Pre – Columbian ornaments. We reminisced of the short trip in the summer of 1964 to Mexico and Mexico City where we stayed with her aunt and uncle on the Paseo de la Reforma and saw similar artifacts in the Museum of History and Anthropology. Good times and good memories! I asked

Mariah if she was ready to go back; she shrugged her shoulders and said, "Business to attend to here first my dear goy!"

That was it for that day with dinner on our student budget being wonderful pastrami sandwiches, cheesecake, and a cold beer in a delicatessen not far from the apartment at Columbia. I was full of questions about life at Harvard and Mariah 'fessed up that she got "hit upon" regularly by colleagues in the Law School, Jewish and other. No surprise, for her incredibly good looks plus smarts! Even a professor or two had asked her if she needed any extra help outside of class, offers carefully not accepted so as not to offend. Like me, life mainly was class and study, and she was thoroughly happy getting this chance to rest from routine and see "the big city" once again. Oh, and heritage!

The Portuguese – Spanish Synagogue

Portuguese – Spanish Synagogue Plaque

The next morning it was back to the west side, Eighth Avenue by the park where we visited the old Spanish – Portuguese Synagogue. I get all the subways mixed up, but I think it was the C line. Mariah knew the right words to say to the watchman at the door (it was not time for any services, so the Synagogue was officially closed) and had pulled a yarmulke out of her small pack for me before we got to the door ("You don't look so bad, but I still see that receding hairline!"). She explained the different rooms, the one where the reading of the Torah takes place, all in gorgeous dark wood, and we read the plaques in an ante – room which told of the Synagogue's amazing history – back to her Sephardic roots. This place was founded in 1654, the oldest in New Amsterdam with Jewish refugees from Brazil! That was familiar to me knowing Jews were "disinvited" from Brazil at that time. Problems and rivalries in the Jewish population in New York caused the people in 1654 to move worship to a synagogue in lower Manhattan and this one on Central Park West would only come into its own later. Mariah was moved emotionally; I just sat and held her hand.

Metropolitan Art Museum

From there it was the cross-town bus to the Metropolitan Museum of Art. We had both seen the Prado two years before, but this was equally impressive and maybe easier to handle, more cosmopolitan in its collection. I won't go on, but there were smidgens of the Italian, Dutch and Spanish masters, however, unlike the Prado, great displays of the famous French modernists, impressionists. We got a bus back over to the south end of Central Park and decided to do the slow walk down 5th avenue all the way to Rockefeller Center and St. Patrick's Cathedral.

St. Patrick's Cathedral

I can't begin to remember all the places but noticed Tiffany's, DeBeer's, two large old Protestant Churches, and finally down to St. Patrick's on the left and Rockefeller Center a bit to the right. They were ice skating in front of that huge skyscraper still in this cold late March. St. Patrick's seemed a bit gloomy to me, dark inside, a lot of scaffolding for painting, I guess. It did not quite come up to those huge cathedrals we had seen in Spain. Oh well.

Just a few blocks over to 9th Avenue and in the 50s we visited a spot colleagues at Brown had told me about – the BEA or Brazilian Endowment of the Arts – a very small operation but with a terrific location. Begun and maintained by a Brazilian ex – pat, Dr. Domício Coutinho, it was "home away from home" for Brazilians in metro New York. The Center sponsored cultural events of all kinds, music, literature, and even a local soccer team. Dr. Coutinho was enthusiastic about my studies and said he hoped there would be a chance in the future, once I had concluded studies, to do a return visit and give a talk on research. We shook hands and left it at that.

Maybe best of all was a real "Irish Pub" next door where we had a quiet lunch and a Harp or two, Irish music on a quiet p.a. in the background and the bartender with an Irish Brogue. Ah, this is what I thought New York should be all about. Dark wooden paneling and tastefully placed Irish scenes on the wall. Someone told me later that "Irish Bars" are not necessarily Irish connected, and there are probably five hundred of them in the city. We had just missed St. Patrick's Day, too bad.

The rest of that day and morning of the next was a bit more tourism, the C train way down to Lower Manhattan, Wall Street, a long walk up through the theater district and famous 42nd street and a quick visit to Carnegie Hall. Late that p.m. Mariah and I had dinner near the apartment. I had no idea of that part of the city, Columbia, Barnard, CCNY, and Fordham up the way – wow – a plethora of hoity – toity places to study. At dinner the night before we had talked of the respective challenges of school, and I'm thinking the grind of Law School was a lot more difficult than what I've already described for me. To each his or her cup of tea. This was spring break and we tentatively planned for a joint trip back to Kansas in the summer to see family, Overland Park and out to Abilene. I asked Mariah if she thought we had made the right decision; after all, we were happy in Abilene those three years and felt fulfilled helping kids at the Juco and being close to family. It was the small town and its limited possibilities that had caused the thinking, at least in part, to do graduate work. But, in love? Yes, and "neighbors" in school.

3

A SURPRISE AT BROWN

So back to Providence and Boston and a lot of hard work to finish the term. Then came one of those events that change your life. It was maybe a week later, after classes had resumed, that Dr. Skidmore motioned for me to stay after class for a chat. The ensuing conversation floored me. "Mike, you have been a terrific student and I think you are on the right track for a wonderful career either in academia or maybe the State Department. The Ph.D. or even a Master's will prepare the way. I just wanted you to know that there is a big change coming up for me. I just received 'an offer I can't refuse' – it is a transfer to Harvard next year to head their Latin American Sector. I won't go into details, but it is 'win – win' anyway you look at it, pay, prestige, research funding and stimulating colleagues. And between you and me, a much livelier setting academically, a bit less isolated than Providence, Boston after all.

"But there's another reason I want to talk to you. Mike, I can easily arrange a transfer of your NDEA Scholarship to Harvard. I'm including and asking two more of your colleagues as well. This by the way is quite common in Academia, after all we on the faculties want the best students. The idea in your case is to give us both a chance to continue your trajectory of study. You will still be in the doctoral program of Latin American Studies but shifting the emphasis to History and Politics. And if you toe the line, work hard, I will be around to chair your Ph.D.

committee. I know this is a surprise, even a shock, so think it over the rest of today and tonight - I've got to know tomorrow. It's late in the term and it can all get done, but haste makes waste my friend. Oh, and keep it all under your hat, word will get out soon enough I'm leaving Brown, but I want everyone to hear it from me, not student gossip. Okay?"

"Professor, in my wildest dreams did I ever think I would be enrolled at Harvard! It truly is too good to be true; Harvard for me was never ever a consideration. Pardon me, this is a 'no – brainer!' Just let me know what to do, paperwork and all. And I shall keep my nose to the grindstone, heh heh. Oh, can I still do a minor in Literature? I'm thinking six courses, three from Spain and Mexico and three from Brazil. Switching to History and Politics will be great, I've always been more akin to Area Studies than to Literary Theory anyway."

"Maybe make that four Lit courses; you've got a fair amount of catching up to do in the History and Poly Sci courses, but with your undergraduate degree and language/ lit work so far, you will have the balance I and many of my colleagues like. Great! I'm glad you are on board; I'll give you instructions as we go along."

The first thing I did was call Mariah who was duly impressed and happy for me, "Hey, there are lots of possibilities, and, uh, distractions. I guess we can worry about that later." She was full of questions and I did not have many answers. As I would find out more, I would pass it on. The next six weeks marked a lot of very hard work, not only attending classes, but doing final papers and prepping for exams. I haven't said, but I did have my car, that Chevy I bought back in Abilene two years earlier, so when term ended, I packed up all my belongings, and headed north to Boston and Harvard where there was incredible (and surprising) graduate housing including parking, a rare commodity. Professor Skidmore had oiled all the hinges, setting me up as an NDEA Fellow in the Department of History – Political Science, and the secretary already had arranged a "suite" (not exactly) in one of the graduate residence buildings - one bedroom with private bath and a tiny kitchen and a small all – purpose dining – living room. Work would get done at a desk in the bedroom. Pretty spartan living, not as nice as at Brown, but who's complaining? My possessions were books, a few clothes, my Sears – Roebuck Classic guitar and a Smith – Corona Electric typewriter. I haven't mentioned yet, but school attire at Brown actually was similar to what Harvard would expect - long sleeve dress shirts, a few ties, a sport coat or two (I had a navy-blue blazer left over from Rockhurst), three or four warm sweaters, dress shoes, and a pair of winter boots.

The soon to be retiring head of the department welcomed me in what amounted to an entry interview, saying as long as Tom Skidmore wanted me, Harvard would not argue with that. Dr. Skidmore would be my adviser and already had me set for a strenuous future in grad school – one course in Brazilian Literature, a Graduate Survey of Latin American Politics, and three history courses, Brazil, Southern Cone Countries, and Mexico. He would be the prof in two of them. Harvard and NDEA take care of their people so I had a small summer stipend for a five-week advanced Portuguese Language Course, board and room in my graduate student housing, and travel for one trip home to Kansas. After I had settled into the "apartment," I saw Professor Skidmore just shortly on campus in the History office.

Widener Library, Harvard

His main comment, "Have you been over to Widener Library yet? That's going to be your 'home away from home.'" He chuckled at this.

4

INTERIM TRAVEL TO OVERLAND PARK AND ABILENE

Mariah was finishing her courses June 6th and now it was easier for the two of us; I would stay at the Harvard apartment and we would take off from there on a trip home together. She had left her car in Overland Park at her parents' house. I couldn't believe all her stuff, even though she was leaving most of it until next term, the fall term; my stripped-down Chevy was full for the cross – country road trip to Kansas City. She was so relieved to finish exams that she said Boston and us would have to wait and was ready to jump in the car and get away from it all. We took a slow three days to get to Overland Park and had lots of time to talk as well as renew the love affair.

We decided to make a b – line as far as Washington D.C. for the first stop. We did not get away until mid – morning, drove down 95 on south toward D.C. It was a harrowing freeway experience but with Mariah in the shotgun seat with good maps and me white – knuckled trying to stay out of trouble with the traffic, we made it to the outskirts of west D.C. by mid – afternoon. We stayed way out west intentionally, but not far from a subway stop. Kind of bad timing on our part, there was not enough time to see some of the sights on the Mall, so we decided they were not to be missed and we would do it the next day. But we did go ahead and take the subway to Union Station and walk to what they say is the best Irish Bar in Washington: the Dubliner. You could see the Department of Justice up the Hill on the left, the Capitol office buildings, and the Capitol itself, and just a bit of the domes roof of the Library of Congress.

The Dubliner on that Saturday was not nearly so busy, but busy enough. I have never been to Ireland or its pubs, but this felt like what I had dreamed of: dark wood paneling, the smell of corned beef and cabbage, advertisements for Harp, Jameson and of course Guinness. We were able to get a booth, order beers and I ordered a corned beef without the cabbage (ugh!) and fries, Mariah said I needed my vegetables, too bad. It was too loud to really do much meaningful talking, but we did hang around for raucous Irish music and two or three more beers. No problem: the subway would take us home to the suburbs. D.C.'s subway was sparkling compared to New York, well – lit, no graffiti in the cars or on the walls. Nice.

Mariah was "decompressing" from an exhausting finals' week, but we managed to have some pleasant time for the romantic reunion. And talk. There would be much more the next three days to Overland Park, but it was interesting and a bit of a surprise. Mariah had weathered the traditional little sleep - all study of first year law and anticipated very good grades. She was however not overly enthusiastic about Law School itself, Torts and the rest. And she intimated, or maybe hinted, that maybe it had not been a good idea. The reader may recall she did finish her M.A. in English the summer before Law School. We would talk about it all on the way to Kansas City, but not yet, one more big day on the Mall in Washington.

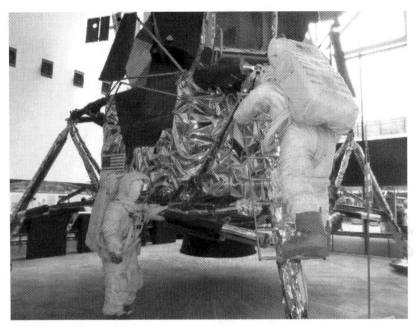

Lunar Landing Module

Ever since I was a little guy, I loved airplanes, drawing pictures of Sabre and Thunder Jets versus Russian Migs in the dogfights in Korea of 1951 in penmanship class in grade school. And one of the highlights of growing up on the farm was the same year in 1951 with a huge flood around Abilene and the locals parking their Piper Cubs and such up on the hill out at the farm. I got my first airplane ride from one of them. I'm getting at my excitement to see the Air and Space Museum on the Mall, the old DC 3s, the fighter jets from WW II and of course the Space capsule of astronaut John Glenn. And the Lunar Landing Module.

The Natural History Museum with the dioramas was great as well, the paintings in the national art gallery less so for me (the Prado two years' earlier with all the Spanish Masters was my cup of tea), but Mariah loved the latter and knew all about the French Impressionists and Cubism ("and no suffering Catholic saints and Jesus"). After that long day we hopped the subway back to the motel and were off early the next day driving southeast away from all that traffic in the East to see the west side of the Appalachians and on through the mountains of West Virginia and then the blue grass farms of Kentucky. I loved the lushness and beauty of the latter, a lot different from wheat fields in Kansas, and we did see some Thoroughbreds in the pastures. We then angled up to St. Louis, crossed the "Big Muddy" and spent a night in its famous Gaslight Square before our last day on the road, rolling into Overland Park the next afternoon.

Before that however in the four hours' drive to Kansas City we had that talk about school, us, and the future. Whatever we decided, it would not happen until after Abilene and Overland Park visits. I was scheduled for that Intensive Portuguese Language Course at Harvard for six weeks from July 1 to August 15th and Fall term would not start until September 15th, so we had some time to play with and maybe decisions to be made.

I say that because Mariah revealed once again that her heart was not really into Law, not because of the hard work, she could handle that, but the vocation itself. I guess I was lucky, or unlucky, knowing exactly what I wanted and how to get there (but easier maybe because I had no aptitude for other things). Mariah had great memories of the teaching in Abilene, the great rapport she had with the students especially the young ladies who saw her as a role model, and her love for English and English and American Literatures. She just had realized then that she did not see living her adult life in a small town. She admitted to some guilt for Dad Benjamin and Mom Ariel's sacrifice to help with the big time first year in Law School and expense at Harvard (notwithstanding a partial scholarship), not wanting the year's effort to go down the drain. Brother Josh already told her there would be a place in his Law Firm, just to give him the word. She had an M.A. in English. What to do? She said she wondered what she could do to add to her credentials to help students *outside* the classroom. We both had done informal counseling to prepare students to apply to the big, four – year schools in Kansas, and that did not require another degree, just our own research. She was a natural; I'm not sure what training or education would be needed to further that, but she said she would look into it. But a decision would have to be fairly soon; after our vacation, it was back East for me and a question mark for Mariah.

5

FAMILY VISITS AND UP TO THE TETONS

The visit with Ben and Ariel was pleasant enough, both pleased at our decision for graduate work and happy to see we had survived the first year. Ben recalled the hellacious first year in Med School back at Northwestern – the all -nighters, too much coffee and too many smokes (hmm, future Doctors of Medicine). They were much the same, Ariel as nice and gracious as ever, Ben inviting me once again to dust off some of those old Hispanic Sephardi books in his library! (Ha! Ha! I begged off saying, "Can they wait for a while?"). Ben took the hint, smiled, and said something about appreciating the really good things in life. I think we did that later, enjoying good food, a concert down at the new KC Arts Center, and Josh and Mariah had a talk about the Law and possibilities (private, Mariah said she would fill me in later.)

Flint Hills, Kansas

The 150 mile drive out home to Abilene was nostalgic enough, having driven it all through college days and more, especially the Flint Hills with its green pastures, groves of trees and beautiful cattle, and we both were moved to recall events from those three years at the Juco and agreed to go up to the college and say hello to Dr. Halderson. Not a bad idea to keep in touch even for professional reasons. I don't want to go into any unnecessary unpleasantries, but Mariah and I talked of the KKK vandalism at St. Andrew's, the farms, and of course the Eisenhower Center. Mariah after a bit said, "Enough already. I'd rather remember your Mom and Dad, the great visits to the farm and around town, and those hot and heavy dates to the supper club in Salina! And the Juco. It seems like a long time ago." We would stay at the new Holiday Inn Express north of town next to the Interstate but would spend plenty of time with Mom and Dad, Ron and Caitlin and see who else was around to talk to. I guess that would mean Wally Galatin down at the 3rd St. Tavern, and hopefully some of our old friends, and like I said, a visit up to the Juco. We allotted three days before a ten-day private road trip up to the Tetons and Yellowstone and then back East.

It was a wonderful reunion with Mom and Dad, trading news, mainly ours; Mom and Dad had never spent time back east (except Dad's just going through on his way to Merchant Marine duty in WWI). Newport and the mansions, Boston and New York, it all seemed pretty exciting to them, and they of course wondered what was coming up the next year. Mom said, "We've missed you. We really got used to having you here. Are you still 'just friends' or is there any news?" "Hey, Mom, I'm just 25 and Mariah's the same. No rush. We'll let you know." Not much consolation in that, I think. Dad just smiled, not saying anything, but repeating that he liked having Mariah help out in the farm garden.

Ron and Caitlin were fun, giving us a bit more detailed version of Mom and Dad, aches and pains, but plugging along. It was much the same situation with Ron's dad and mom on the farm out on the Smokey Hill River south of town; both sets of parents were of the same generation with the same pew seating in church. Now with four kids, the oldest six, Caitlin had a handful.

The big news was at the Juco, or I should say, the former Juco. Professor Halderson greeted us, alerted his secretary to hold his calls and closed his office door to avoid interruptions and brought us up to speed.

"Mike and Mariah, we have missed you dearly. There is big news - the Dwight D. Eisenhower Community College has received state approval to become the newest four – year state college in Kansas! Our enrollment has grown each year, by the way, no small thanks to the two of you! We will be the 'new guy on the block' but with at first just a few possible majors: English, History, Psychology, Liberal Arts Science, and Business Management. No language majors, but the students can get a 12-hour minor in Spanish or French. The news just came one month ago. With the state's blessing it will mean a significant increase in funding and in hiring. While we won't be able to compete with the big three – K.U., K – State and Emporia State – we will be a good alternative. A four – year bachelor's degree opens many doors. The competition will be the small four year largely Church Colleges scattered all over Kansas, and we will now be a strong candidate for the graduates of the two – year junior colleges. I don't think the Church Colleges will be too upset, because in truth it is the church affiliation and religious training that appeals to most of them. I'm hoping we can reach the 1000 student enrollment this coming Fall. Actually, one large classroom building, an addition to the library, and another dormitory – cafeteria building will do the trick, but no small task to be sure. No plans yet for clubs or athletics, but I surmise people will clamor for that.

"I turned 60 a month ago, and am thinking that in five years, all things being equal, I can get this well off the ground. Our location, the beautiful town of Abilene, the need for a college that is not so big and scares off many students, but most of all the name and connection to President Eisenhower should stand us in good stead. You two by the way are on my wish list. What is your news after one year in those fine graduate schools back East? Students still miss you, and I get calls to bring you 'home.'"

I went first, briefly reporting on life at Brown, but mainly the invitation to start at Harvard in about three weeks (Dr. Halderson beamed) and Mariah then chipped in with her take on it all. She was forthright (I thought) on the year at Law School, but that also she was unsure of what course of study to continue. She asked Dr. Halderson about what *he* thought most young people needed help with outside the classroom.

He was quick to respond, "Someone with no personal agenda to mentor them, someone to let them know they care, sometimes just an adult to talk to. So often these kids are from broken homes or out here in Kansas with parents who have no college education themselves. They need an educated, helpful friend."

"How do you study for that, Dr.?"

"You do and you don't. It's that simple. There are guidance counselors in all high schools, thank God for that, and they are instrumental in sending us many of our students. I have met a couple dozen of them over the years and talked to more on the telephone. But they almost always have another discipline that they teach, and in high school counseling is a duty 'bestowed' on them like sponsoring the cheerleaders or maybe the debate team. If they have a professional degree, it is usually in Educational Psychology, Psychology, or Communications. I would say the main qualifications are, pardon me, like the 4-H Motto, 'I pledge my head and heart to better living.' If you don't mind my saying, Mariah, you were doing a perfect job at that when you were here. I shall go out on a limb and repeat what I said a year ago, if both you and Mike want to come back here, I will personally find a place for you. Pardon me once again, I don't think a Harvard Law Degree is essential; your Master's in English would suffice, and if you want to do more graduate work, we need solid teachers and not necessarily publishing scholars. Psychology would be the ticket; you could teach both disciplines and become what we could call a College Advisor on the side."

"Thanks, Dr., I'll look into it and see what good ole' Harvard might offer with some transfer credit from the Law School. I mainly have to do some hard thinking the next few weeks and see if I can find some direction."

"And Mike, what an incredible opportunity you have ahead of you. We could use a Harvard grad for the History Department, and you already have the Language preparation. I get excited just thinking of it – prestige for our new college, topflight teaching, and a local boy. Just give me the word."

"Doc Halderson, you asked what was new and we've told you, but I think it will be two years at the most before either of us would be prepared for what you've talked about. I'm personally open to it, but a lot can happen. Thank you for being so kind."

"Well, like I say, I think maybe five more years for me here before retirement, so don't wait too long. I see your parents in town, and Ron and Caitlin, and we always have time for a chat, so we can all keep you apprised of changes in town. Times are changing, the country is growing, albeit with the turmoil overseas, I mean Viet Nam, and I want us to be a part of it, the growth I mean. What is changing most is farming, a serious subject; it is clearer than ever that we have to prepare the high school graduates to go on to something other than taking over the family farm. In 90 per cent of the cases that isn't feasible anyway."

"Oh, I did not mean to forget it, what about you two? Providence is not that far from Boston, and now, both of you in Boston! So what does that portend? I assume you are still an 'item'?"

I think Mariah blushed, and I stammered a bit. "Dr., yes we are indeed an 'item.' We have not really discussed any changes this coming year, but I guess we will figure it out." Mariah nodded her head.

We bade our goodbyes, promising to stay in touch. There was another stop or two in town, one with Sheriff Wiley; when I called, he was extremely happy to hear we were in town (word gets around) and invited me down to the office, including Mariah in the visit. I warned Mariah about his lousy coffee, and so warned we sat down to a very interesting conversation. That office brought back lots of memories, not all pleasant. Wiley welcomed us saying he was just a country boy and all that business back East – he had never heard of Brown but had heard lots about Harvard – was kind of like a fairy tale to folks in Abilene. How were we doing in the big city? He associated Harvard with rich folks and the Kennedys in politics. We both assured him that we would not be there if not for some healthy scholarships, and I added that the best of Juco students could indeed dream of it!

Talk moved on to family, his wife and two sons doing well, the older boy whom I knew fairly well in Abilene just a year behind me now in graduate school himself, but down at K- State for Agricultural Engineering, and the younger doing well at ole' AHS. He politely asked of Mariah's family and she gave the short version of her Dad doing well as an M.D. in Overland Park and Mom with social duties and brother Josh in a successful Law Firm.

"What about you two? You 'gonna get hitched? That was the talk in town a year ago."

We repeated the "just friends" mantra but that we still were very much interested in each other and probably would see a lot of each other next year in Boston. But then, I wanted to turn the conversation to those harrowing days of the bombing at the Eisenhower Museum now almost two years ago and any news on all that. Wiley, never one to mince language and pretty down to earth with me, knowing he could rely on discretion and a closed mouth, launched into about a fifteen-minute update. Here's what I remember:

"Mike and Mariah, you would never know much of anything had happened from just being around town now. They redid the west side of the Museum and the sidewalks and parking lot in short order. The Museum and the Library and the new Chapel are all open for business. All the surrounding places, St. Andrew's, the Santa Fe Train Depot, and a few houses in the neighborhood were all taken care of pretty quickly by the insurance companies, broken windows and the like. And the Santa Fe replaced those twisted tracks and runs a tourist train to Enterprise and back these days, in cahoots with Old Abilene Town and tourism.

"Those, pardon my language Mariah, sons a' bitches who did it are doing hard time down at Leavenworth and I suspect will never see the light of day outside those walls. If the damned jury had called it first degree murder, we would have electrocuted 'em. But, manslaughter was decided, Joe Weston being in the wrong spot at the wrong time. They were out to do property damage (recall the bomb was set to go off after working hours). Well, maybe. (He harrumphed at that.)"

"Wiley, I'm just as interested to know your take on what happened later up in Idaho, the ATF and FBI raid on the separatists and KKK camps and the violence, bloodshed and deaths that resulted (in June 1966 for the reader who has not read "Rural Odyssey II – Abilene Digging Deeper"). We only learned about it via newspaper clippings mailed to us and your phone call."

"Serious business Mick and Mariah. It was armed conflict and although no law officers were killed, three were wounded, and there was intent to kill. The bastards rounded up are doing life sentences in the federal prison in Idaho, and the compounds were broken up, we understand most of the people moving on up to Canada. Fine with me, but I don't trust any of 'em. If anything, people like that have long memories and will be out for revenge whenever and wherever they can take it. It's the damned mindset – 'Us against them. And no goddamned government is going to tell us what to do.' Hell, if it were me, I'd deport 'em all to South America and let 'em start a revolution down there. But this time they are not fooling around with just Abilene and the law and courts here, but the *federal government!* That's a whole other deal.

"The KBI, in coordination with the FBI and ATF, gives us regular reports on separatist activity and behavior, and that includes not only Idaho and Montana, but all over the country. There is no activity in Kansas now or even in bordering states, so I'd say we are relatively free of it, but it's still 'watch and wait.' I sure as hell did not or do not mean to alarm you, but damn, Mike, you know firsthand what those folks are like."

Sheriff Wiley would talk to me later in private revealing further thought, saying, "I didn't want to alarm Mariah' especially since so much of all this is speculation. I think the whole damned USA should be on alert."

I said, "She is probably as tough as you when it comes to trouble, things her family has had to put up with for generations, and sure as hell is tougher than me."

"You did all right buddy boy; you can ride shotgun with me anytime. Just be sure that snub nose 38 is full loaded next time and you've got an extra clip!" He laughed at that.

Like up at the Juco, he wondered if we would be coming back to Abilene, and we repeated what I've already said, maybe two years before we would or could make any decisions. "Don't wait too long or we'll all be pushing up daisies and you'll have to go back to the cemetery to take pictures of us."

Another visit was over to St. Andrew's where we caught now Pastor Father Kramden after doing a funeral that morning. He smiled, said my

Dad had been a mainstay in the volunteer work, and that you would be surprised how many deaths required extra pall bearers. And he patted my shoulder, "Mike, I tried to get you to seminary in High School, but I'm happy to see how everything has turned out, and especially happy to see Mariah once again. It is good you two are still on track." We talked just a short while, saying the Abilene visit was short, but would try to check in either later in the summer before Fall term or perhaps during a vacation this coming academic year. He blessed us both.

The last visit was, well, down to the tavern on 3rd street and a good talk with Wally Galatin the photographer specializing in Eisenhower days, all our conversation over 25 cent Coors drafts. You always had to be a bit careful with Wally because anything at all you said would be fair game for local gossip. So, we did not mention any particulars with Dr. Halderson or Sheriff Wiley, but just that we had checked in and had good talks. He was totally apprised of Ike Eisenhower's affairs, now fully retired on a farm near Gettysburg near the family ancestral home and a place in Palm Desert California where he could play golf. Wally's own photo book on Ike in Abilene was well along and he wanted to know what my loose-leaf notes on "History of Abilene" had come to. I just said it was all tabled for the moment but did say I would be doing History and Political Science at Harvard in the Fall. "That calls for another round, maybe the Harvard guy should buy!" I did, that cost me another 75 cents! We said goodbye hoping for an encounter soon. There was no meaty gossip shared although Wally knew it but just did not get around to it. His main comments were that the town seemed to be slowing down, still with major tourism, but farming showing a slump. That would be a topic for later.

After a final and bit teary visit to Mom and Dad, we took off on that road trip to the Tetons and Yellowstone and then the long drive back to Boston. It was meant to be a break from academia, and it was, among other highlights, past the Flaming Gorge in Utah. The reservoir backs up the Green River almost 90 miles north all the way into Wyoming. Spectacular views from the dam itself. Then we drove through the barren plains in Wyoming, saw not as many antelope as we wanted, but car camped in the plains below Jackson where they used to have the frontier rendezvouses. That was when we saw the surprise, an entire herd of antelope (my favorite wild animal), then the Hoback River and drive into Jackson. It pushed our budget, but we found a motel room on the way out of town south, made it into the main square with all the elk and deer antlers above the sidewalk, and even made it to the famous bar where you sit on saddles instead of stools and famed for a Willie Nelson concert. A beer and a hamburger and fries went down well with the country music.

Next a.m. after a terrific breakfast at a famous local place, the Bunnery, where incidentally we got to speak Spanish with the waitress originally from Guatemala, it was out to do the drive around the park which took most of the day. We got our fill of buffalo, antelope, deer, a fox or two, and even three black bears, but the highlight was the Tetons themselves; neither of us had seen them. Awe inspiring and unforgettable. And the rivers, especially the Snake. We got a tip from a ranger and parked near a small tributary to the Snake and saw a huge beaver pond with huge beavers (I could not help thinking of the rage of beaver trapping and the beaver – skin stovepipe hats of 100 years ago, and what almost wiped the beavers out). And now in mid – June there was evidence of the summer bird migration, warblers, grossbeaks, and the like. And to my pleasure a few migrant Western Meadowlarks like in Kansas.

Supper that night was at another famous place, Dornan's Bar and Pizza with huge plate glass windows with a magnificent view of the Tetons before dusk. It was along there at a crossing called Moose that we saw a huge full racked bull in the stream up to its ears with moss hanging from its mouth! We understand he's a regular, maybe in the pay of the local Rotary Club. After an early dinner of pizza and local "Moose Drool" beer we did the drive around the west side of the park and saw herds of elk, and in one of the ponds a Kingfisher diving and catching fish! We actually had to dodge some animals, mainly buffalo and deer back to the motel in Jackson. We decided this place deserved at least a week, but … another time.

Old Faithful, Yellowstone

Next morning we did the drive north, passing for miles the Tetons on the left, and then the Rockefeller Parkway into Yellowstone. We saw our first geysers but saved the best for that afternoon – Old Faithful and the crowds. I admitted it was great as was the walk on the wooden boardwalk around the geysers, but in my mind Yellowstone did not match the Tetons for the scenery and the animals. However, the lodge at Old Faithful was something else. Mariah had wangled a hard to come by reservation for that one night. The room was tiny, a bit worn, but comfortable, but we had never seen anything like that immense perhaps five story lobby with the huge stone fireplace in the center, the log stairs and railings and then the huge spiderweb of log beams surrounding the lobby and supporting the roof. We got ice cream and then coffees and just sat in the easy chairs on the second floor overlooking the entire scene. And listening to the babble of crowds from all over the world. It felt good to be an American!

6

BACK TO BOSTON

The trip was not what I would call leisurely, but we did manage to stop at some sights; there were others I don't even remember. We drove to the Black Hills and Mount Rushmore with the stone sculpted presidents, angling on down to Mt. Pleasant, Iowa where I wanted to see the famous steam tractors and farm implement museum, just one day in Chicago to see the sights around the lake, skirting Toledo and Cleveland, and then all the way across Pennsylvania, taking the jog up to Scranton, and then across Connecticut and on up to Worchester and Boston. Whew! Mariah and I talked about all we had seen in the big, wide world and how fortunate we were at that young age – Kansas City, Abilene, Mexico City and the Pre – Columbian sites, Spain, Providence, Boston and New York and now what has to be among the best in the west of the U.S.

I think you could say indeed that we had had our break from academia, and now it would be back to work. No question for me, the Advance Intensive Portuguese Language Institute at Harvard right away in July and the Ph.D. courses in the History – Political Science program in the Fall, but for Mariah it was a bit more complicated. In the end she decided the Ph.D. program in English with a minor in Counseling (but still thinking of the old concept of Guidance) would set her up for either high school or college or university programs. Since she already had the Masters in English and had done psychology on the undergraduate level, they calculated two years and two summer schools would take her to the stage for the Ph.D. in English. Same as me in two years. That is, and a big proviso, if all went well. There was really no way to transfer the Law School credits except for the fact her fine academic record prompted Harvard English to offer her a fellowship for the advanced degree. Wow! She was greatly relieved, happy her parents would not have the financial burden; she would not have to try to work part time and could get on with it.

That left her and me. I think we had this conversation out in the middle of Pennsylvania. I would be 26 in August and Mariah would follow in November. We tried to discuss all the what ifs. Big ifs. Would we get married in a church or a synagogue? There was no question either asked or answered for either of us converting to the other's religion; I think because both of us were beyond orthodox religion of any kind. By a priest or a rabbi? Both? Do we want children? Do I follow the old custom and rule and say the children, if any, are to be raised Catholic? Jewish in Mariah's case? It isn't as though this was the first time a Jewish girl married a Catholic boy, or vice – versa, and things were known to work out just fine. How would our respective families take all this?

And there was the other matter, perhaps more immediate: Do you love me? Do you love me enough to spend the rest of your life with me? When would we get married? What about school? What about jobs after school is finished? We debated the pros and cons of Abilene, still with Dr. Halderson and now a four-year college. Was that ambitious enough for either of us? Are there or will there be other options? What does each of us really want out of life? Is money, family money or income a factor? That's enough to take you from New York to Los Angeles, much less Pennsylvania to Boston.

My god, I think we talked until Connecticut and then tabled it. Seemed like a re – run of June a year ago when leaving Abilene for the East. Unlike many couples of those changing times, Mariah and I had never "lived together," but we surely had a lot of "test runs" and time together, the occasional night in Abilene, times in Mexico in 1964, in Spain in 1965, and sporadic time since. Neither of us doubted our compatibility, our joy of being together. And our love; we cemented that once again that night in the motel. I won't get into all those answers, but just say we were both on the same page, just the big matter of when! For better or worse we decided to be together at each other's place in Boston at Harvard, but not move in together, switching places each weekend for variety. And seeing where we were with it all the next June. I guess educational goals trumped it all.

It was probably a good decision; the rest of that summer was the most intense academically we had ever experienced, just getting "caught up" to continue the Ph.D. classes in the Fall. I haven't said much about the national and international scene, but things were heating up, the aftermath of the Civil Rights Movement and Law of 1964, the continuing escalation in Viet Nam, the ensuing draft and war protests (40,000 in Kesar Stadium in San Francisco) the Beatles continuing popularity and the space race. That's just for openers.

7

YEAR TWO – BOSTON –
FALL 1967, SPRING 1968

Time moved fast because we were so busy. I can name just a few of the on and off – campus events that were simmering below the surface - the carryover from the anti – war protests including a confrontation between the SDS and Defense Secretary McNamara last year. The Seven Day War in Israel and Egypt had taken place that July of 1967 and changed the entire course of the Middle East. Brazil's Military had moved into full dictatorship mode with General Costa e Silva, but not before a "terrorist act" at the Guararapes Airport in Northeast Brazil in Pernambuco took place in July when an attempt was made to bomb the plane carrying "new" President Costa e Silva (by consensus of the hard – line generals ruling the country). All the latter was duly noted by Professor Skidmore in my classes.

I was quickly discovering why Harvard was so highly spoken of, particularly in this just my tiny part of the University that Fall. The contact and interaction with major scholars and writers was a reality at that place. Aside from Thomas Skidmore's classes and guidance almost daily on campus, there was a major Visiting Professor who changed my academic life – the writer Carlos Fuentes from Mexico.

I had read two of his important novels as an undergraduate, "Where the Air Is Clear" ["La Región Más Transparente del Mundo"] and

"The Death of Artemio Cruz" ["La Muerte de Artemio Cruz"]. The first chronicled life in Mexico City in the late 1950s, mixing Mexico's Pre – Columbian past with its dynamic present through the narration of a "pesero" taxi driver on Avenida Paseo de la Reforma. The second novel was much broader in scope really chronicling Mexico from the 1910 -1917 Revolution which changed the country up through the turbulent post – war times of the PRI ("Partido Revolucionario Institucional) and strife, albeit in fiction but history accurately remembered. He was considered "An Intellectual Dandy" by his main rival in Mexico, Historian Enrique Krause, and was a known leftist sympathizer of Ortega in Nicaragua and other leftist causes in Latin America. But he also was a highly talented novelist espousing daring literary techniques and styles of the "Latin American Experimental Novel" of the 1960s. I don't know the agreement he had with Harvard, thinking he did not teach regular classes, but he did give monthly lectures and guest lectures in different classes.

I attended them regularly as did anyone interested in Latin America, professors or students, and had a chance to ask a couple of questions based in part at my short time at the National University of Mexico [UNAM] in the summer of 1962. This led to a mentoring situation in coffee – clutch gatherings later when Fuentes awoke in me and provided invaluable hints for the study of Mexico's folk – popular culture seen in the ballads called "corridos" and woodcut art by José Guadalupe Posada who illustrated many of the same broadside ballads at the height of the Revolution. Fuentes also encouraged me to study the role of the Mexican Muralists, especially Diego Rivera and then Frida Kahlo as the most important feminine voice in Mexico. He also guest - lectured in my graduate literature class on the "Experimental Novel of Latin America" that fall in Cambridge. This would lead to a Harvard Summer Fellowship for four weeks in the summer of 1968 to Mexico with study in Mexico City for the work of José Guadalupe, the broadsides and the "corridos." More on that as it comes up.

The second big awakening to Latin American Literature was my survey course of Brazilian Literature in the Spring term of 1968. It opened my eyes to the works of Jorge Amado, the best – known novelist of Brazil, and in the same class, almost by accident, study of the corresponding Brazilian "version" of the Mexican "Corridos," the broadsides of what Brazilian folklorists called "Popular Literature in Verse" or "A Literatura de Cordel" ["String Literature"]. The latter had many similarities to the "corridos," several of its major themes dealing with current events, politics, national heroes, and love and scandals in its "newspaper in verse of the poor." Antônio Silvino and Lampião the bandits of Northeastern Brazil were chronicled like Emiliano Zapata and Pancho Villa in Mexico, and the course of 20th century politics was traced as well. "Cordel" however also brought the re-creation in verse of the European Epic Hero of Charlemagne and popular successors in Brazil.

And a further sign of the times – drugs, marijuana, and flower children. So much was happening in America. The "Summer of Love" and the flower children in San Francisco was morphing into the Counterculture Movement, and flowers were associated with confronting bayonets in the anti – war demonstrations. But there was a scientific corollary taking place at Harvard at the same time. Professor Evan Schultes had studied magic mushrooms and morning glories' hallucinogenic components as far back as the 1940s in Mexico, and Peyote in the Southwest, followed by study of the rubber plants in Mexico during the crisis of World War II. This led him to his wide reaching ethno – botanical studies in the Amazon and his amazing life experience with native peoples and founding of the Harvard Botanical Museum for the study of the same that put him on the map at Harvard. Curare and ayahuasca studies were no small part of the groundbreaking research. He saw all those plant producing drugs in their context of use in native medicine and religious rites all over the Americas.

Needless to say, growing up in the 1940s and 1950s in Kansas, and as an undergraduate with the Jesuits in very early 1960s had not prepared me for this, a whole new world. Fortunately, study trumped the drugs for both me and Mariah. We did attend one of Professor Schulte's lectures on plants and medicinal uses in the Amazon, a whole new world after El Dorado. They didn't find its gold, but evidently there's a "new" gold in Colombia.

Meanwhile, Thomas Skidmore and others led us to in – depth study of American History, Latin American History, History of the Spanish Southwest, and of Mexico and Brazil. This did not all come at once but would be spread over intense courses for two and one – half years. Politics of the respective areas was always a necessary part of each course. I was studying what I loved and had dreamed of studying since undergraduate days. In short, I was "a happy camper."

Mariah was equally immersed in her program. She had done pre – requisite courses in Psychology and Counseling in the summer and was now into advanced courses in American Literature, dividing time with that and the minor in Counseling. An entire seminar on the southern writers, Faulkner the head of the list but an introduction to a future eminence, Flannery O' Connor of Georgia, was a topic of our conversations. Mariah in addition was delving into Jewish writers, and there were many, Philip Roth the predominant figure. I wasn't much help but did "lend an ear" to her musings. I could not identify with Roth at all, but she did. And Faulkner was too "deep" for me, a real contradiction because the "Stream of Consciousness" techniques were certainly instrumental in Carlos Fuentes' novels. Flannery O'Connor was another story. I told Mariah, "Those characters and that language and colloquial speech could have come right out of the Kansas I grew up in." She agreed with me saying just the three years in Abilene seemed to jog her memory on that as well. She admired Flannery's inventiveness, but her background and blood drew her to a fascination of Roth's fictional telling of Jewish life especially in the 1960s.

Related but unrelated, there was a scary bit of news from Ben and Ariel in Overland Park. In those turbulent times of unrest of 1967, red swastikas were painted on the wall on the front of his practice and those of half a dozen other Jewish doctors in Kansas City. Ben calmed us both saying he thinks it was an isolated moment, probably related to the Civil

Rights' Struggles and Law of 1964, Jews being connected to blacks, foreign immigration, and the battles for civil rights as interpreted by the racist, white minorities. And Ben recalled the significant KKK presence in Kansas City, Kansas back in the 1920s. There is a famous photo of a large KKK gathering in that place, the KKK people in the white robes with hoods, all mounted on horseback in a huge parade. Police investigated but no one was arrested.

So never a dull moment, well, mostly. Mariah and I both might have been accused of having our heads buried in the sand because there was only one real priority – studying and doing it well. And us. A topic I forgot to mention until now, related to college study – I had a draft deferment on the undergraduate level for college study, granted by the local Abilene, Dickinson County Draft board in 1959. I didn't ask for it but was given it. (The reader will remember my Dad and both brothers were in the military and I played 'war games' up in the silo with brother Paul's Korean War plastic helmet liner on my head, binoculars, and bayonet on my belt.) I'll never know the why and wherefore of all that, but I think at that time in farm country going to college was considered a worthy goal to serve the nation. Several of my friends got the same deferment. But at Harvard in the NDEA program, there was an automatic deferment; the National Defense Education Act was seen as a major effort to train future scholars and teachers to teach others about the "at – risk" areas of the globe in the Cold War against the Soviet Union. Spanish and Spanish America, Portuguese and Brazil were cases in point. So amidst all the turmoil and anti – war protests at least I did not have to worry about being yanked out of school for Viet Nam. As time passed and passes now, I'll address this again. But I can say that back home in Abilene, they don't like draft dodgers. I was never accused of it and once again I never consciously thought about it, but I surmise that doesn't mean that I was never talked about. In my mind I was serving my country in the best possible way, preparing others to contest Communist aggression in the Americas. I was doing a lot more than I would have done trying to carry that 80 lb. pack in Army basic training on a 15-mile hike, but I admit the idea of it made me feel uneasy. Most of my high school buddies who did not go to college volunteered in 1959 for the service, and being a Marine was considered the ultimate goal.

Another big event that year was another guest lecture, this time by Skidmore's "out west" connection – E. Bradford Burns of U.C.L.A. who had the best history book out on Brazil with that title, "History of Brazil." We of course all attended the lecture and his guest lectures in the history classes. How can I say this? I would never but never have been exposed to such people except at a school like Harvard. And the old cliché proved true: Harvard opens doors! I really don't know how you could top that first year. And more than anything else it created an atmosphere, a mindset, to strive for excellence. As Mariah never tired of saying, "Farmer boy, you're not in Kansas anymore! And neither am I." I would attend lectures in her department as well, some renowned literary critics, but confess my head was turned toward Mexico and Brazil and not to the "Harvard Literary Review."

We did see a lot of each other, and there were intimate moments in respective apartments on the weekends. Entertainment was beer and pizza in local student hangouts, lectures by the people I've been talking about and an occasional concert (Harvard got comps for graduate students to the Boston Pops Concerts), or movie. Not too intellectual, I remember taking Mariah to "From Russia with Love" with Sean Connery at the local movie house near campus. I kidded her, "Good looking, you could have been that Bond girl in Istanbul!" "Whaddaya mean? Didn't I tell you they wanted me to audition for the part?"

Union Oyster House, Fanueil Square

There were two or three times downtown at Faneuil Hall, the Boston Oyster House and the Irish Pub next door. I tried the oysters, but one was enough. Slithery, slippery. Mariah, more adventurous, did her half-dozen, and we both quaffed a cold Boston Lager.

Maybe the biggest entertainment moment that first Fall in Boston was a Saturday afternoon at a place I only saw on TV growing up – I mean Fenway Park and the Green Monster. It was Harvard connections once again and two tickets in the bleachers above the Green Monster for a game with an unnamed team in last place, but still hard to get tickets. Unnamed: the bottom dweller Kansas City A's. Mariah grew up a fan of the Kansas City Athletics, the vagabonds moved from Philadelphia by crazy Charlie Finley (he of the yellow uniforms and even yellow baseballs in spring training). I wrote somewhere else that a bunch of us Abilene High School buddies went to K.C. for a weekend and I got to see Mickey Mantle smash a home run and Moose Skowron and Tony Kubek, all of course of the visiting New York Yankees, in the Katz drugstore downtown near our modest hotel. But Fenway Park, wow! Two weeks later Boston won the pennant but sadly went on to lose to the St. Louis Cardinals in the Series. But I did see Carl Yastremski and Rico Petrocelli do their thing. We had to drink a couple of Sam Adams Lagers at prices our budget barely could handle and of course a couple of hot dogs. I had my Kodak Instamatic and have a dozen pictures for posterity. The scarier moment was riding the subway from Harvard all the way out to the Back Bay and the park, all with lots of raucous can I say rowdy fans.

Mariah and I were both able to get cheap (that is a relative term) red – eye flights to Kansas City during the Christmas Vacation and flew together. We got a taxi from KC Municipal to her house in Overland Park and had her car to get around town some and for three days out to Abilene. We missed Hanukkah but did get time with Ben, Ariel and Josh. Everyone of course was anxious to hear news from Boston, the academics and us. And us from them. There were no more anti – Jewish surprises, all calm at the practice and life as usual. We all trooped down to the Plaza with the terrific Christmas lights, recalling the visit back to Sevilla two years ago and to that same delicatessen of times past. Mariah and I had nothing to announce, and her people were all using discretion in the matter, that is except for Josh. "Hey, you two are not getting any younger. (Ha ha). What's new? Mom's thinking of wedding plans and Dad's writing letters to the Vatican for a dispensation for Mike for a nice Jewish – Catholic shindig."

Mariah said, "None of your business, smart ass! You'll be the last to know."

I said nothing; what could I say?

The drive to Abilene on that same Interstate (by the way, done by Eisenhower in his years and clipping 20 acres off the north end of Dad's farm, Imminent Domain you know) but through the Flint Hills after Topeka, was like another world in winter. Everything was brown and the temperatures were just above freezing, no cattle now in the pastures, but we did hear a storm might be coming in around Christmas, and maybe some snow. The short stay in town was mostly about family, visits to Mom and Dad, Mariah and I buying and putting up a small, live tree "for old times' sake" at the house, presents opened on Xmas Eve, and, are you ready, Mariah going to mass with us all Christmas Morning, a first. She told me, "Don't make anything of this; I'm doing it as a gift to your Mom. I know none of you are to blame now, but what the Catholics have done to the Jews the last five hundred years is not water under the bridge." She said later she was impressed with the singing of the small-town choir with bits of the old Gregorian still sung, and Father Kramden had a good voice. I got in line for communion (but no earlier confession) and there was no lightning bolt; I believe God indeed is all knowing, and he and I had our private moment before mass. There were not quite as many of the old folks I knew there, but I did recognize some faces, and I think they all took notice of Mike and his female friend. Mom and Dad seemed very happy at the latest turn of events.

The snow came a day later and a lot of it, enough to put on boots and warm clothes and tromp around the pasture out at Caitlin and Ron's. Ron and his brother Stan and Mariah and I went rabbit hunting, a real hoot in the snow. You basically follow the tracks to where they are hunkered down, let them run and "kaboom" with the shotgun or 22 Special. I didn't get any but Mariah the old sure – shot bagged three. Stan took them home to skin then and have rabbit stew. Before Caitlin's big dinner there was all the hullabaloo and excitement of Christmas gifts and the four kids. They started calling Mariah "Aunt Mariah" and we all got a kick out of that. (Mariah said later, "It makes me feel like an old lady. Jumping the gun there a bit methinks.") There was no big news to discuss, lots of farm news, and everyone wanting more details of Boston, Harvard and the East. We filled them in, me embellishing the Fenway Park outing some, and big city stories of the subways and Paul Revere's Last Ride. (Some details corrected accurately by Mariah, "Farmer boy, you should be ashamed. *I'm* not the history major.)

We did not try to get all around town again, but promised we would try to get back next summer some time, schedule and schoolwork permitting. We drove back to Kansas City the next day, had an evening with Ben and

Ariel and took another red eye for Boston later that night. We both agreed it was a good break. Harvard was still on a semester system, so we would face exams and then a two – week break in January. We each had two term papers left, so those two weeks were kind of like the week from hell.

8

WINTER AND SPRING
IN NEW ENGLAND

I was not wrong, both of us burning the midnight oil for exam prep, me in a literature course and a history course, Mariah in that American Lit course. Term papers were handed in, and grades posted early, all A's for Mariah, me A's and one B. Who cares! You can't win 'em all.

What else? This was the second year in New England with those winters. The key was warm clothes, lots of sweaters, a good heavy coat, stocking cap, gloves and especially warm boots. There was a humungous blizzard in all New England that February. We walked on the Boston Commons more than once with beautiful flakes coming down. We were ready for another break, so we joined all the other crazies to drive up to Vermont and do a couple days of winter skiing at Arlington.

I'm a beginner and a klutz, doing the snowplow to stay out of trouble, Mariah a "medium" with some former experience while on a trip with her sorority girlfriends from K.U. a few years ago, plus being more athletic. The good news – no broken bones – the less than good news, we both caught colds and were ready to head back to the residences in Boston to nurse them. We did stop in Arlington to see a very small museum of Norman Rockwell "Americana." That was cool, memories of the "Saturday Evening Post" covers from growing up, a mainstay on the farm.

Back at Harvard, we cozied up together at Marah's place for hot soup, some TV and lining up books and all for spring term.

I was excited, more great stuff coming up: History of Mexico, Brazilian Literature, and History of the U.S. Southwest. Mariah was due for another course in English Literature, this time on Shakespeare, a big order, and a graduate Counseling Course. Now used to the "drill," it was easy to settle into routine. But things soon started to happen. As that calendar turned to 1968, I don't think anyone could have imagined all that would come, even with all the signs of unrest in 1967.

In that same late January, the Viet Cong started what would become the Tet Offensive, making the war, the protest and tension increase all around for everybody. The nightly news became the nightly horror show: the body count of casualties in Viet Nam, and the next protest and/or riot in one of the U.S. cities. I privately wondered about one thing – does this prove the validity of the NDEA program and in my case getting ready to teach others about critical places and languages in the world, i.e. Spain, Portugal, Spanish America, Brazil? Yes.

Dr. Skidmore was great as ever in a History of the Southwest course filling us in on the push west by the U.S., often called "Manifest Destiny." (General Polk or is it Poke?) We studied all the famous "Trails," the Oregon to the West Coast and the Santa Fe closer to home touching part of Kansas (Council Grove with Dad's relatives, Larned and its fort west of Abilene). I guess I found most interesting the "Camino Real de Tierra Adentro" Trail that Spain did before Mexican Independence, from Mexico City to silver rich Zacatecas and up through the badlands in New Mexico all the way to Santa Fe which became the outpost of Spanish influence in present day New Mexico. (Maybe I was enamored of this not only for Spanish and Latin American Studies but the fact my first Spanish Language Textbook in high school was entitled "The 'Camino Real,'" me not realizing at all the significance of the same). We learned the ins and outs of the U.S. – Mexico War of 1846 to 1848, the facts plus the folklore (the "independence" of Texas in 1837 with Davy Crockett and the Tennessee

Volunteers at the Alamo and General Santa Ana). The bottom line: Mexico lost approximately one – third of its national territory to the big bully from the North and never but never would forget it! Imagine: California, Utah, Nevada, New Mexico, and Arizona! The U.S. added insult to injury with the so – called last straw, "El Chamizal" affair on the Rio Grande between Juárez, Mexico and El Paso, Texas when the Rio Grande changed course in the U.S.'s favor. It was finally settled by treaty only in 1964 with Presidents Lyndon Johnson and López Mateos of Mexico. Of course, the well substantiated argument on the U.S. side was that Mexico never had the resources to develop all that land, or the will perhaps, and we did. Okay.

I discussed with Professor Skidmore a "History of Abilene" as a tentative future dissertation project, and we both agreed there was plenty of history there to deal with, a topic tabled yet for another year. "But if you have any spare time, ha ha, you could begin to look into it." He said maybe I could tie in the topic of Mexican – American participation in the cattle drives from Texas and the building of the Kansas Railroads around Abilene. And always of interest would be the Santa Fe Trail through Kansas, and my interest in the "Camino Real" Trail up to Santa Fe. All the above related to Spanish and Spanish American studies.

So, Spring Term rolled along rapidly mainly because we were so busy. By now Mariah and I were truly "old friends" as well as sometime lovers. There was the occasional disagreement or spat, but nothing serious, and I think we were settling into something more permanent, yet to be determined. We were happy to get news in April of a replay or whatever you want to call it that would come in the summer, this after our second year in graduate school. I got a summer extension from the Harvard NDEA for four weeks in Mexico to research topics already mentioned related to the graduate studies. Mariah got a small grant of $2000 from Harvard Counseling to look into how the Mexican Ministry of Education handles counseling for prospective college entrants. Her uncle and aunt David and Sara Palafox invited us to stay with them, but we declined mainly due to the length of our proposed stay. David responded with arranging a two – bedroom apartment for us on Calle Londres in the Zona Rosa just a few blocks from their house on the Paseo de la Reforma with the proviso that we visit once a week for dinner and socializing, "an offer you cannot refuse." It would be a great adventure.

Before mid – June when we would travel, the stuff had hit the fan while still in classes in Spring Term. Lyndon Johnson declared he would not be a presidential candidate for a second term, this in March. Someone in the press said it was because the national news icon we all trusted, Walter Cronkite of nightly CBS, came out against Viet Nam and the war. I wondered if the nightly body count, and U.S. soldiers' prisoners' count got to him. Johnson said something to the effect that if he lost Walter Cronkite, he lost all of America's middle class. Maybe so. Martin Luther King was assassinated in April and massive national black protests and riots followed. Ironically, Lyndon Johnson signed into law the national Civil Rights Act of 1968 a week later. I don't think it was much consolation at the time, but eventually all recognized King's actions as well as all the events stretching back to 1964 as seminal to it. Just before our departure Robert Kennedy was killed in Los Angeles on June 5th during a campaign trip. My God, when will it all stop?

King's Chapel, Boston

We did not travel during Spring Break, too much work to do, but did manage to get around a little more in Boston. One place was that impressive but seemingly "out of place" downtown on the way to Faneuil Square, King's Chapel. It had caught our attention when we learned that Evan Schultes of plant fame in the Amazon had attended church there. Originally New England Anglican (WASP country) it now was affiliated with the Unitarian Universalist Church, the latter of great interest to us. The old Neo – Classical building stands next to shiny skyscrapers in the old downtown.

The more you investigated Boston, the more you found, all really overwhelming in the history of Colonial New England and the beginnings of the U.S. I guess our visit to the Old North Church had to be on the list. Legendary scene of Paul Revere's last ride warning the citizens of British attack in 1775, the lantern hung in the belfry as a warning, and the battles of Lexington and Concord, be that as it may, it impressed me far more on the inside which really revealed what the original New England Puritan worship was like. It was Episcopalian originally, and ironically, many of its worshipers remained faithful to England! The stark simplicity of the place but most of all the small, individual seating "pods" or squares designated for each family remained in my memory. There was a small choir from I don't know where singing a Capella hymns when Mariah and I were there. Beautiful.

And Mariah insisted we even it all out with a visit to an incredibly beautiful and important former synagogue, the "Blue Hill Avenue Shul" of old days in Boston. Adath Jeshurun was a spectacular place of worship in Roxbury, that is until the changing times and Jewish migration out of the area. It became the Ecclesia Apostolic Church in the same days as our visit and the old, beautiful building is in the process of being restored. We took lots of pictures both outside and inside, a moving experience for both of us.

Spring term came to an end, term papers and exams, and both of us really excited, we embarked on a reprise of sorts to Mexico, including a brief visit to family in Overland Park and Abilene before the Mexicana flight to Mexico City in mid – June. The reader may recall from "Rural Odyssey II" that we visited Mariah's aunt and uncle David and Sara in summer of 1964 and had a wonderful "quick" tour of colonial and pre -Columbian Mexico while enjoying their hospitality. We talked of the different plan this time on the three and one – half hour Mexicana flight: research for me on the "corridos" and "calaveras" of José Guadalupe Posada, and the frescos of Diego Rivera and self – portraits of Frida Kahlo, and Mariah at the Ministry of Education, but regular dinners and visits with her relatives.

9

MÉXICO DE NUEVO

Nothing like starting out at the top: Mariah's uncle Dr. David Palafox sent his chauffeur in the Mercedes sedan to pick us up at the airport. He and Sara were in the car when we arrived with luggage. Lots of warm "abrazos" – "Cuatro años! Quién hubiera pensado?" ["Four years ago! Who would have thought!"]. On the drive into Mexico City and to their comfortable home on the Paseo de la Reforma there was time to catch up just on the basics - Benjamin and Ariel and Josh doing fine in Kansas City, my parents the same in Abilene, but Mariah and I *both* at Harvard! That was interesting to David and Sara, as it would be to most upper-class Mexicans. David remarked off the cuff, "Yes, and that 'dandy' Carlos Fuentes has been hanging around up there earning accolades and big dollars!" I did not then make a big deal of knowing him fairly well, not talking of his lectures and our own conversations and he one of the main reasons I'm in Mexico now. Better over drinks when everyone was a bit more mellow. (The reader may remember the Carlos Fuentes – Enrique Krause animosity of past times in Mexico, Krause, Jewish, a Palafox family friend.)

They were pleased Mariah and I were still an "item," but Sara restrained herself and put off more questions until later. David's company of medical supplies and equipment was booming as was his practice. "More later when we get home. You'll see a lot more construction in the city since

1964, mainly because we have the Olympics coming up this Fall, a big affair. And traffic is worse than ever. Let's get home, get you settled, have a welcome drink and we can continue the conversation." As usual, I was in a near state of culture shock with the immense city, the traffic, the noise, and yes, the smog. Summer rains were expected and would soon cleanse the air of this the city that Carlos Fuentes called the city "Where the Air Is Most Clear" in the 1958 novel. Ha, ha in 1968. I was happy to see the old red jalopy "pesero" taxis still on Reforma; David said it's now 10 pesos! And the "Ángel de la Independencia" just two blocks away from their house.

After being ushered through the tall iron gate of the masonry wall in front of their three – story stone mansion hidden behind a virtual "forest" of tropical plants, whisked to our rooms (ahem!) on the third floor and instructed to come down for coffee, tea or cocktails (it was now close to 5 p.m.) before dinner, we all settled in the large drawing room with a cheery fire going in the seven-foot-tall stone fireplace. David remembered I enjoyed a good scotch (he had the real stuff, not the ersatz national version famous for giving headaches) and Mariah a nice wine; we settled in for the first of many talks it would take to catch up from 1964 - lots of water under the bridge! Although they were apprised of general events in the United States by Ben and Ariel, they did not know of Abilene events (perhaps due to the reticence by the latter). They did know of national and international events, the assassination of Martin Luther King April 4th and of Bobby Kennedy, June 6th, 1968. And the general turbulence in the U.S. caused by the Viet Nam War – the street and college manifestations. David said the students in Mexico of course always looking for a cause had protested as well in solidarity.

Mariah and I felt obligated to bring them up to date sharing the highlights of what I've already written about it in "Rural Odyssey II," but mainly the bombing at the Eisenhower Center in Abilene, our decisions (unrelated) to not renew at the Juco but go to graduate school (applauded very much by David and Sarah) and events since then. That was when, after two drinks in front of that big fireplace, that I admitted it was upon the advice of Carlos Fuentes that I return to Mexico and study the history and politics in the "corridos" [Ballad – poems of the Mexican Revolution] and the broadsides of Vanegas Arroyo and lithography of José Guadalupe Posada, knowing of course David's opposition to Fuentes and his politics.

"All that aside (Fuentes I mean), Miguel, we in Mexico cannot escape our own history, the desecration of indigenous Mexico by the Spaniards, the turmoil of the War of Independence, the Liberal – Conservative wars of the 19th century and the magnitude of the battles and deaths of our Revolution of 1910. It is just now coming to light how folk culture in the 'corridos' and popular culture contributed to our national culture at least the last 50 years. We all know of Rivera's painting that is in the Hotel Alameda depicting Posada, "La Catrina," and Frida Kahlo of that era, but honestly it is only recently that scholars including literature and art people are really delving into it all. I'll have to make a few phone calls to my 'sources' to help you out – I think Historian Enrique Krause might be a good start. That is, if you would like a little help."

"Dr. Palafox, 'Seguro que sí,'" [Of course]. So far, maybe for the reasons you suggest, major collections of the 'corridos' are more *outside* of Mexico than here, but I think some serious poking around Mexico City may alter that. Enough of that; Mariah has a big project as well."

"Tío David, Tía Sarah, I've done a bit of a turnabout since first year Law at Harvard; I'm back to what I think is my true love (she looked over at me, a glance not unnoticed by our host who smiled) – English and American Literature, and Counseling Studies to formally help future students. I have a Masters in English and in one more year at least the ABD [Academic parlance: All But Dissertation], so we'll see where all this goes. I plan on teaching and advising Hispanic students as well in the future, so I thought perhaps Mexico's methodology on all that might give me a clue or two. I've got letters of introduction to Agustín Yañez from my Harvard mentors and am hopeful I can get the Ministry of Education as an avenue in my research. It could lead to the dissertation topic as well."

"Caramba! Mariah! We know Agustín and I think your friend Miguel should tag along. Like the candidates for most political jobs in Mexico, writers are well thought of and in high demand. It is no different at the 'Secretaría de Educación' [Ministry of Education]. Sr. Yañez wrote one of our most famous 'Novelas de la Revolución,' 'Al Filo del Água,' ['At the Edge of the Water'] and I'll bet he knows as much or more about 'corridos' and Guadalupe Posada than most people here. We know him because he actually is a patient or mine, and I daresay I helped him through a medical crisis. He has been eternally grateful, so I'll give him a call."

"Gracias, Tio, I suppose that will help along with the letters. Maybe Mike can go with me one day and see all those murals Diego Rivera painted at the Ministry. But he knows *this* is *my* research and we shall keep both separate."

There was a bit of a silence, then David laughed and said (all this is in Spanish by the way), "All of this research business is on the periphery – we see Miguel and Mariah again. What about you two? We have been thinking a lot about that especially since we got your news of a return here to Mexico City. It has been almost four years, who could believe it? We don't see engagement rings, is that too forward? Please satisfy our curiosity. Sarah will chide me for saying all this, but I don't care."

I looked at Mariah, she blushing a bit but with an answer that did not offend me. "Tío David y Tia Sarah, las noticias son buenas! [The news is all good.] Miguel and I have chosen to remain friends, very good friends at that, take things a year at a time, and both fulfill our goals of graduate work. But perhaps we are more in tune with the customs of the 'new way' of handling all this, although I suspect it is much the same now with young people of our age and circumstances in Mexico, made public or not. We have always had separate apartments wherever we live, but how do you say, 'with visiting rights.' Ha ha. (David smiled, Sarah looked down a bit.) And it will be the same for these few short weeks in Mexico City, one apartment, two separate bedrooms. Miguel is the love of my life and I am sure that one fine day you will be getting that air mail, special delivery notice of the big day, but not yet. Am I right, Mike?"

In spite of all our talks, our plans, our time together, I was taken aback, but managed to blurt out, "Sí querida, de acuerdo completo y bien dicho. ['Yes, dear, completely in agreement and well said']. We never have desired to be apart, and both are looking to the future. Which I do believe is getting closer!" I stood up, walked over, planted a kiss on her sweet lips, and then sat down beside her.

Sarah stood up, said "That's good enough for me. Congratulations. I more than David have wondered about all this, but am happy to say, as long as the flame burns, good things happen. I know your plans are not formalized, but we shall try to be patient. Maybe David and I can convince you to really have a special 'luna de miel' [honeymoon] in our Mexico!" She gave Mariah a huge hug and maybe just a little less huge for me.

David seconded the motion and said we should get ready for dinner, the boys would be over, and we would have to repeat all the news for sons Jaime and Lucas, Mariah's cousins (the reader might remember them from "Rural Odyssey II"). A few minutes later, the big front door opened, and two very handsome young gentlemen came in, both making a big deal of hugs for Mariah, more formal "abrazos" for me, Jaime blurting out "O' Gringo Viejo'que placer verte de nuevo y saber que mi prima loca Mariah todavía tiene ganas de estar a tu lado!" ["Oh, Old Gringo, a pleasure to see you again and to know that my crazy cousin Mariah still likes to have you by her side!"] Lucas, always the more polite and reserved cousin, said, "Me da mucha alegría verles de nuevo. Para mí, no es ninguna sorpresa! Los dos se ven tan bellos y todavía jóvenes como la última vez." ["I am really happy to see you again. For me, it is no surprise! You two are as handsome and still as young as last time."] "Of course, of course," Jaime said, "Aren't we all?" It turned out to be a great reunion, another drink of scotch in the big living room, lively conversation, much laughter and then all moving to the formal dining room for a scrumptious what I would call banquet of Mexican specialties.

Over garlic shrimp, rice and vegetables, and "veal parmigiana a la Mexicana," champagne and a fine wine, and flan with caramel sauce, the evening turned boisterous and maybe a bit loud for Doña Sarah! There was news – Jaime is engaged to a beautiful Mexican señorita (but incidentally also Sephardi of an old Mexican family), Raquél de León, the wedding set some time before Hannukah. "Sorry, Miguel, that you could not be here for the courting and the proposal; I hired the best Mariachis all the way from Jalisco to do the serenata when I popped the question. Fortunately, Raquel said yes." Applause and toasts by all. Jaime by the way, a Business Management graduate of the "Colegio de México" is on the corporate ladder of one of the largest "grupos financieros" of México. I don't think we have to worry about the future of either of the Palafox boys. Jaime added, "I think you two will be in the middle of school and classes for our special day, but maybe you can send the gift special delivery! (Ha ha)."

Talk the rest of the evening moved on to discuss our research projects, Lucas taking the lead in filling us in on what we might expect. He, after all, was tuned in to Mexican culture and cognizant of the deep roots of the Revolution yet in modern history. He offered to accompany us on a revisit to the Rivera murals in the National Palace and to the Ministry of Education if need be. David interrupted there saying, "I think Don Agustín will want to do that personally." Jaime said, "Perhaps we can all go to 'Los de Abajo'; it's the best place for real Mexican chile, 'corrido' singers and drinking tequila the old – fashioned way – salt and lemon and down the hatch! None of this 'fine liqueur' folly in vogue today. Believe me I know."

I said, "We'll let you know. Sounds like fun. Do I take my big sombrero, a guitar and a 'pistola'? Ha ha. I would like to go ahead and go to the Hotel del Prado tomorrow and back to the National Palace and see the old and new murals. Maybe in a day or two we will hear from Secretario Agustín." Don David assured us he would move quickly on the phone call and request and was confident Agustín Yañez would move us up on his appointment list (unsaid, if he wants to keep getting good medical advice).

The night ended after more conversation with Mariah and I exhausted from the travel. Oh, and Don David said our apartment on Calle Londres was waiting for us; he personally requested that we allow him to show it to us, meet the staff (!) and settle in. Wow!

10

SETTLNG IN AND THE DIEGO RIVERA MURALS

That did happen the next morning. Accompanied by the chauffer in the Mercedes we arrived at the walk – up apartment with a great location in the Zona Rosa and a short walk either to Reforma (to get the "peseros") or to Insurgentes (more "peseros" or the bus). The apartment was not fancy, but was very comfortable, a small living room with divan, easy chairs, a TV, a dining room with a view to a small kitchen, two small but comfortable bedrooms, each with a writing desk and a good lamp (a good thing in Mexico) and the bath. We were introduced to Mercedes – housekeeper, laundress, cook and great teller of stories of her "pueblo" in Chiapas near San Cristóbal de las Casas. Mercedes was "on call" for guests whenever. We clicked and would leave her a very generous "honorarium" upon our departure. But what a location, walking distance to the Reforma and Insurgentes, and a longer walk to Chapultepec (I would take Mariah to that zoo I loved back in 1962). It all made me think of my host family then, living somewhere close I think; I looked but could not find their place, to them I am eternally grateful.

After lunch back at the Palafox residence, "tour director" Lucas accompanied us to the historic center, to the Alameda and the Hotel del Prado – the goal, Diego Rivera's famous mural. He wanted to go in the

Mercedes, but I convinced him to join us in a "pesero" ride (Mariah had vowed to never get in one again after last time in DF). "Sólo esta vez, verás que el vivir en México es muy peligroso. Cuidado, eh?" ["Just this once, you will see that living in Mexico is very dangerous. Careful, huh?"] Fortunately, we weren't mugged, the car did not break down and we got a colorful commentary of life in DF by the "chofer" – "México hoy es una gran chingada, pero qué hacer? 'México querido' como dice la canción." ["México today is all fucked up, but what can you do? 'Beautiful Mexico' as the song says."]

The mural in the El Prado was astounding. It was commissioned for the Hotel del Prado's dining room, the Versailles Room, in 1946 and it took one year to finish. Jaime said it has many of the figures of Rivera's "Historia de México" in the stairway of the National Palace in the Zócalo, in this case 150 characters! Hernán Cortés, Benito Juárez, Maximiliano de Hapsburgo, Francisco Madero, Porfirio Díaz, Frida Kahlo, Porfirio Díaz's wife and daughter are just a few. But it is the center of the mural that was most interesting to me, a real homage to José Guadalupe Posada. It shows the famous engraver arm and arm with his main creation "La Calavera Catrina," and a young Diego Rivera as a boy to his other side, and Frida Kahlo behind him. La Malinche (Cortes's translator and perhaps mistress) is in a bright yellow dress to the right of Posada and the Alameda Park in the rear. Rivera said of it, "The mural is composed of memories of my life, my childhood and my youth from 1895 to 1910. All the characters are dreaming, some asleep on benches, and others, walking and talking." Rivera often expressed his artistic debt to Posada and called him the greatest of México's popular artisans. Photos of the mural were not allowed, and any images are copyrighted, so the reader will just have to take my word for it, me and tens of thousands of others who have marveled at this amazing, brilliantly colored work of art.

The Mural, Hotel del Prado

We had time to walk back to the Zócalo and the National Palace and see once again Rivera's huge "Historia de México" mural, just for comparison. I wrote all about it in "Rural Odyssey II" three years ago. Each mural on successive walls of the palace stairway depicts epochs of history of Mexico – pre conquest, conquest and colony, capitalist domination until the Revolution of 1910 and then the Workers' Era. The mural in the Hotel is smaller, easier to manage, brighter and certainly more akin to my current interests, but these latter were really given a boost via Mariah and my fortuitous visit with Secretary of Education and major novelist Agustín Yañez, that bit of good news awaiting us that evening when we had dinner with David and Sarah, Jaime and Lucas.

We had drinks in the "sala de estar" [living room] again, and then a sumptuous dinner. Conversation was stimulating with lots of laughter and quips from most all of us. Jaime, the businessman got a bit serious, saying, "If you will pardon me, Diego Rivera (may he rest in peace and his commie wife Frida Kahlo as well) was a Marxist and would gladly throw us all out of our house here on Reforma if he could come back from his tomb; I'm just glad the PAN [Party of National Action], the pro -business, centrist - right party here is really getting into a position to throw the corrupt PRI [Institutional Party of the Revolution] out. Most of their ideas are political blather from fifty years ago, and Mexico's only way forward is with progressive business measures and the global economy. Our young star Vicente Fox (no relation to the Palafox name) from Guanajuato and an upcoming politician who happens to be currently manager of Coca – Cola International is someone to watch."

This caused a visceral reaction from brother Lucas, "Jaime, if your crowd takes over Mexico, it will be the end of us all. There will be no compassion for the masses of poor people, health needs for them, education; only the rich will be happy and get richer."

Don David at that point intervened, "We did not raise you two to be at each other's throats, especially in our dining room, a little healthy discussion okay, but I think this is going in the wrong direction. For you Jaime, the PRI in spite of all its cronyism, has brought Mexico what it needed most – stability – and that's why your financial people have the freedom and opportunity to grow the economy. The PRI evolved from ten horrible years of war, genocide, and even fratricide, and for all its faults and inherent socialism, is responsible for your opportunities today. And Lucas, no one party no matter who will solve our economic ills of class, land holding, and discrimination in Mexico. But you are right in that PRI has provided a safety net, no matter how imperfect."

Lucas still was not finished, "Communist or not, no one, and I mean no one, has depicted Mexican history and national life better than Diego Rivera, and if the elite would get off its high – falutin' pedestal, they would see that the same can be said of José Guadalupe Posada and the 'corridos' and broadsides he illustrated."

Jaime blurted, "If you mean skeletons and the 'Día de los Muertos,' ['Day of the Dead'] está bien."

Don David interjected, "I think our guest Professor Miguel may be able to enlighten us all on that at least in a week or two. Mariah and Miguel,

I heard from Don Agustín, you two have an appointment at the Ministry on Tuesday, so get your ducks in a row; he is a busy man. You've got homework Miguel, a thorough reading of 'Al Filo del Água,' ['At the Edge of the Water'] and Mariah, you need to check out the Constitution of 1917, the important clause on public education for all in Mexico, and the role of the rural schoolteachers. I've got it all in my library. Two days should do it."

I think both Jaime and Lucas were not finished but reached a truce of sorts, Jaime saying he was prepared to take us and his "socialist" brother to "Los de Abajo" (named after a famous revolutionary novel "The Underdogs") tomorrow night if for no other reason than to prove he really does appreciate Mexican "country music." "Ha! The surprise will be you will get to meet my fiancée Raquel. This will be a night of what everyone calls 'México Lindo.' I will pick you up at 8 p.m. and take you to the club which happens to be next to one of the biggest Mexican theaters where they have 'variedades,' on Avenida Juárez, and we can get our fill of that whole scene." Lucas added we need to get to a good "variedades" show as well, plenty of time.

11

"LOS DE ABAJO" - A NIGHT OF "MÉXICO LINDO"

So all went just as planned, that is, except for one change: Lucas respectfully bowed out, thinking the two couples would end up having more fun. Jaime picked us up at the apartment a little before 8 p.m. on that Saturday and we were off to "Los de Abajo" bar – restaurant – club. When we got in the back, Jaime turned to us and introduced Raquel de León, his fiancée. She was a dazzling dark brunette, and it turned out, vivacious and a bit feisty – like Mariah! We would get to know her better later; we agreed to do that soon since it was not a great night for personal conversations at "Los de Abajo." Introductions were made in the car, and then Jaime "prepped" us on the place. It is a combination ballroom, bar and restaurant, a real "down home" place for Mexicans more than tourists to have a taste of their musical and gastronomic heritage. Tables are set around the dance floor and the Norteño bands played (there are several, each succeeding the former, based on different northern and central states of Mexico). Waiters and waitresses are in Mexican cowboy attire (not mariachi, this is different), and many in the crowd the same – the men in cowboy boots, blue jeans, plaid shirts, some with kerchiefs, and a felt or straw cowboy hat; the women in jeans as well, but so tight it made me think of the hillbilly song growing up - "Baby's Got Her Blue Jeans On" and how she stops traffic in her country town - tops that showed off their assets, and cowboy hats as well. We noted there were hefty bouncers ["cadeneros"] at the door, and Jaime said, "If you get out of line here, be prepared to land headfirst on the brick sidewalk in front."

"You don't drink bourbon, scotch or wine here; it's 'tequila con sal y limón' or Mexican beer (I knew some of the brands from 1962 days) – Dos Equis or Superior." That allowed me to tell my student anecdote from 1962: after returning home from the UNAM on the bus, I would stop at the corner 'bodega' and buy a Superior for one peso, drink it right there and smoke a cigarette before heading home to my host's house. Jaime said, "You are a wild one, aren't you? Did you try our national version of Lucky Strikes - 'Delicados,' Aaaah!" I said, "No Jaime they smelled like something from the fireplace. I was into Marlboros." And that allowed me to tell of a college job when I gave out free packs of Ligget and Myer cigarettes in the college dorm until no one would take the damned things. The job gave me $25 per month, all the cigarettes I could smoke and the habit it later took years to get rid of.

So we all started off with a ceremonial shot of tequila – lick your left hand between the thumb and forefinger, sprinkle on salt, down the shot and lick the salt. Wow! I also knew from experience (at El Tenampa, a dubious nightclub on Plaza Garibaldi that both Jaime and Lucas were familiar with) that one might be enough. I switched to beer, and in fact so did everyone else. The waiters came, a hunk of a guy for the girls, a real beauty for us guys, and told us the menu – no written menu here. "Mar" or "Tierra", mounds of fried shrimp and fish, with rice and beans, or a combination plate of taco, tostado, tamale, and rice and beans. Salsa and chips, hot tortillas with the meal, but no salad, and then flan for dessert.

We all ordered, and they kept the beer coming. Piped 'norteño' music was on until 9 p.m. when the show and dancing started. We were wearing jeans and plaid shirts, minus the cowboy hat, so blended in some, after all, two real Mexicans, one look – alike (Mariah) and one obvious gringo. The dancing was what I would call an old U.S. - like two – step, 4/4 time or 2/4 time. There may have been 'corridos,' but with the blaring volume I could not get enough of lyrics to know, but the sound was unforgettable and great! It's still in my groggy head as I write this. Rhythm guitar, bass guitar (electric and way too loud), violin, but the greatest, the "soundbox," a small accordion with some bands, the full – sized with others. I had learned that all along the northern border with the U.S. and adjacent states that the German musical influence (due to settlers) was significant, so it is. They even have a "shottish" rhythm. You cannot sit still in your chair with this music!

The bands kind of blended into one another as the night wore on, big, handsome Mexicans with black hair, big mustaches (but no beards), jeans, cowboy boots and hat. I think the music was more "música norteña" than 'corridos,' but Jaime did request "La Adelita" and "Valentina," old standbys, the first a two – step, the second in waltz time (Mariah and I sat that one out, "gringos can't dance waltzes"), but at least two dozen couples on the floor were terrific and did not miss a beat. After about two hours, still early in Mexico, we were ready to leave, the music getting louder as the night wore on.

Jaime insisted we not go home yet and took us to the Hotel María Isabel rooftop bar for a nightcap and talk ("Don't worry about your clothes, if I tip the maître-d you could walk in 'pelados' [naked]). It turned out great because we finally had a chance to get to know Raquel a bit better (and vice -versa). I told Mariah later, "So this is how real upper-class Mexicans end their evening? Beats Frank's Friendly Tavern on 3rd street in Abilene. Ha ha." There was soft jazz (are we in Mexico?) candlelight, and we could hear each other talk (except for the ears ringing from "Los de Abajo"). Jaime started, "Well how did you like it?" Mariah and I both said it was a hoot and I said I really felt like I had arrived in Mexico! That was when Jaime 'fessed up: "I have to tell you this was only my second time. For many of our friends it is what you call 'slumming it,' so with the usual crowd we hang out with it's not a regular place. Here at the María Isabel, right now, is more the normal speed, usually late night after dinner at a very fancy restaurant. And also, I'm glad there were no fights earlier on; the place is known for that, but I did not fear for our safety knowing those hefty bouncers were still there."

Raquel spoke up at that point, "I told Jaime he should think twice before his choice tonight, but he said 'No te preocupes, será como las tabernas de los vaqueros de Abilene para Miguel!' ["Don't worry, it will be like those cowboy saloons in Abilene for Mike!"] Isn't that right?"

Jaime responded, "Well, yes, I did say it. But it was a joke. I apologize profusely but Miguel y Mariah if I thought there were any danger believe me, I thought the cowboy gunslinger might be able to take care of himself, but I never would have put you in that position. Did we have fun?"

Mariah said, "Claro que sí. But now we just want a quiet drink and to hear about you two. And Raquel, I think we are already 'sisters' in spirit, so I want to hear your take as well. Ándales!"

Jaime started off, "All right. Raquel is two years younger than I but a whole lot smarter. We met through, surprise, the Synagogue, and connections between the two families, I'm thinking the mothers. We were introduced one Friday evening, the first time I had attended in months, but what's the word, 'encouraged' by Mamá. I thought, 'What's up?' Is this like being introduced by your sister? Or worse, a blind date arranged by your sister? Lucas I'm sorry to say can't play the role. But what can I say? There are hidden jewels upstairs when the Torah is read! This lady was dazzling and gave me permission to call the next day!"

Mariah retorted, "It's true and mostly accurate; you will learn I don't see eye – to – eye with the Shabbat rules, but my mother Dorotea said there would be an extraordinary message that evening. What message? 'An extraordinary message, trust me.' So indeed, Jaime and I were introduced in the foyer of the temple after the services. I gave him permission for the phone call. He called the next day and we met for coffee and Sunday brunch at a 'trusted' café, in fact, Sanborn's. I do believe the cliché – I was swept off my feet by this handsome, debonaire, witty, funny and a bit forward fellow. Of course, I didn't let him know that. We began dating,

Mexican and Jewish style, coffee, movies (preferably Jewish connected, but that's no problem), dinner and dancing. Things evolved; that was two years ago, and so you have it. Oh, yes, I never did find out what the 'extraordinary' message from the Rabbi was. By the way, in case you are wondering, and what else would a Jewish girl (meaning Mariah) wonder, our families are quite compatible, practically speaking, I mean social class, education, and respective roles in Mexico. What could be nicer? (She laughed.) So, what about you two?"

Mariah told her in capsulated form what the reader already knows, still friends, still in love, but on hold for graduate school and degrees. And "We'll let you know."

"Sooner better than later, and a honeymoon in Mexico," said Jaime.

So after a terrific Mexican evening, home to bed and upcoming plans.

12

AGUSTÍN YAÑEZ Y LA SECRETARÍA DE EDUCACIÓN PÚBLICA [AGUSTÍN YAÑEZ AND THE MINISTRY OF PUBLIC EDUCATION]

After getting up late after the "Los de Abajo" outing on Saturday, I spent most of Sunday at David and Sarah's house in the library, reading "Al Filo del Água" (again) and Mariah at the same time was boning up on "las maestras rurales" [female rural schoolteachers) and the basics of Mexico's Constitution, a task her for which her law school days had prepared her well - all the small print and dozens of articles. So that next Tuesday we took a taxi to the Secretaria de Educación Pública and were ushered into Secretario Agustín Yañez's office promptly at 10:00 a.m. He greeted us warmly, saying that we came with the highest recommendation from Dr. David Palafox who had given him an introductory "synopsis" of Mariah and me, our background and research purposes for the short term in Mexico. He ordered "cafecitos y galletitas" right away. He said he had set aside one hour (very generous) for our interview but wanted us to start off.

Ladies first. Mariah explained her degree program at Harvard, Ph.D. in English with a Minor in Counseling (Guidance), wanting to teach in high school or college education but with the opportunity for Hispanic students. She explained her Sephardi background and thus her knowledge of Castilian and Ladino. She wanted to know how Mexico was training teachers as counselors, especially on the college level and wanted to interview a small number of teachers and perhaps visit schools. She said she was quite aware of the main points of the Constitution of 1917, the emphasis on public education, and the role of the female rural schoolteacher.

Agustín smiled and said (all in Spanish of course), "You've come to the right place Mariah. If you will forgive me, I am obliged to 'toot my own horn' a bit, so please indulge me (what else could we dream of doing?). During my term as Secretario de Educación Pública in Mexico, we have made great strides, particularly in the alphabetization of rural Mexico, the training of primary and secondary school teachers, getting resources to the schools, but also, I may say, in Counseling Education. I have pushed for the use of the "vias de comunicación," radio, television, and distance learning throughout Mexico. We have come a long, long way since 1917. My office secretary will set up however many interviews you desire with a selection of secondary and college – level teachers, and I think, with a little push from me, that can start this week. Just give Graciela your schedule and she will coordinate it all. If I may just tell you, a link to the graduate program at Harvard, through you, will be quite beneficial to us; Mexican educators can only dream of Harvard."

Mariah thanked him profusely agreeing with "manos a obra" ["to work"] as soon as possible, and conveying any pertinent information to the Harvard Counseling Department.

He turned to me, "Miguel, Don David has also enlightened me with an introduction to your interests. I have to say they please me equally as Mariah's. Even though my work now for decades has been primarily dedicated to education, I think you know we cannot divorce that from culture and its relation to the history and the ideals of the Revolution and Constitution. I am a long – time PRI man and firmly believe Mexico cannot stray from its revolutionary ideals. You have also come to the right place, but perhaps in a more private way, not generally divulged to the public. For many reasons, some lamentable, I mean the fragility of our archives and library collections, and pardon me, downright thievery. Just for your knowledge today: I have a very respectable personal collection of the broadsides of José Guadalupe Posada including many of the 'Calaveras' [day to day characters as skeletons, a satire on death] and many, many 'corridos.' In fact I used to visit the printing shop in the old downtown 'centro.' That's why he presented me with an entire satchel of old and important broadsides. You may know I am a writer as well and with some modest success in Mexico; it helps on such occasions; still my favorite writing today is 'Al filo del água' and what we call 'La Novela de la Revolucion.' I would like to make a modest proposal to the two of you: dinner at my house this next Saturday night, and a perusal of some wonderful, historic Mexican documents as well as Mexican food and music. And Mariah, I have interacted with rural schoolteachers now for thirty years and have many personal photos and memories I will be happy to share with you. I have to say, Mexico today is modernizing, moving on, really a very different country from those times of my youth and work, and that is a good thing. But it will make me extremely happy to reminisce of those days. I'm hoping David and Sarah can join us."

"Dr. Yañez, we are floored with your generosity, and will be honored to have this opportunity. I don't know if Don David told you, but I was one of those 'gringos' in the summer school at the UNAM in 1962, and you, Señor, visited one of my classes. I knew practically nothing about Mexico and had not read your novel, so it was just this 'famous Mexican' in class. I now can say, Thank you! I read several of the 'Novels of the Revolution' in graduate school the last two years, yours among them, and then the beginnings of study of the 'corridos,' José Guadalupe Posada, Diego Rivera and Frida Kahlo. And a topic we can talk about, Brazil's 'literatura popular em verso' and its version of Posada's broadsides - 'a kissing cousin' of the 'corridos.'"

"¡Caramba Miguel! Con mucho gusto, eso de la literatura del cordel del Brasil, no conozco, y tú puedes enterarme de todo!" ["Wow Miguel" It will be my pleasure, I am not familiar with the 'literatura de cordel' from Brazil; you can fill me in.] All right, my time is about up, is there anything else we can do now?"

"Don Agustín, we would like to peruse the halls here and see Diego's murals. Is this possible?"

"If you wait just two hours, I can accompany you. Why don't you have lunch nearby in the Alameda, maybe even at the hotel and come back at 2:00 p.m. We can do it then."

"Como quiera ud. Estaremos de vuelta a las 2:00."

He came around the desk, bowed to Mariah, gave her a light "abrazo" and a formal handshake to me. I was in a daze, and I think Mariah as well, and we both wondered later what in the world had Don David done to help Agustín Yanez's health; it must have been significant for this warm treatment and invitation. Mariah said she would very carefully ask Don David later; it was probably very private but maybe we could get the 'big picture.' We both were already thinking of questions and topics for that dinner! Lunch came first where we, still euphoric from the a.m. session, reviewed the meeting and congratulated ourselves on our good fortune, in no small way due to "Tío David." ["Uncle David"].

Back to the Ministry, all went according to plan. Don Agustín showed us the way. What turned out to be a quick tour took over an hour, and even that was partial; I had no idea of the immensity and historic value of this set of murals of Diego Rivera. And no idea what we had missed on an earlier visit to Mexico City when we had seen the "Historia de México" murals in the Government Palace. One could spend a month, each day studying a single mural and its value for Mexico. I could tell Dr. Agustín was "in his element," and we marveled at how he could still feel and share the enthusiasm, obviously of a lifetime of work as writer and public servant in Post – Revolutionary War Mexico. Because of copyright complications, I have included my own photos from the National Palace when they at least match the themes of the Ministry.

Diego Rivera Mural, National Palace

Sr. Yañez started us off with a disclaimer, "Miguel y Mariah, Diego Rivera was an avowed Marxist and depicted all his murals with that Marxist Dialectic − black or white, good or evil. The basic concepts of our Revolution and Constitution are indeed Socialistic, embodying the vast changes due in Mexico after three hundred years of colonization and colony and a disastrous 19th century. But we have learned that Socialism alone was not and cannot be the key today to progress in our country; it must be a balance of Socialism and Capitalism and that is what you see today in Mexico. But the ideals of the history and the Revolution are here in one large gallery. I'm going to show you just what is applicable and perhaps easiest to internalize and digest. There are paintings in two spaces:

Diego Rivera Mural 2, the National Palace

1. 'The Work Patio' – 'La Planta Baja' details scenes of work and abuse of workers in Pre – Revolutionary Mexico, the freeing of the 'campesinos,' and Mariah, a scene central to your research – 'la maestra rural.'

2. "And perhaps more important for both of you, 'El Patio de las Fiestas- la Planta Baja,' with murals of national and regional 'fiestas' in Mexico like 'Día de los Muertos' with some of Rivera's most critical murals depicting capitalism - 'La cena del Capitalismo' and 'Banquete de Wall Street,' or 'La Orgía'), the beginnings of conflict and revolution with a major role by the adherents of Mexico's Communist Party ('En el arsenal' and 'Zapata') and programs of the Revolution in the post – revolutionary early era ('Alfabetización'). The communication of

the revolutionaries was seen in the 'corridos:' ('Cantando el Corrido'), and Rivera finishes his entire painted story with 'Fin de Corrido.'

"I think you both will see and appreciate why all this is so important to your research interests. And incidentally, I think I am one of the few Mexicans who have lived through it all and really understand the entire process. I'm hoping we can talk much more about it all at dinner on Saturday."

I spoke up, "Don Agustín, we are eternally grateful for your time, your efforts and your patience. I am sure Mariah and I will be thinking of ways we can promote an understanding (much needed) of Mexico, the Revolution and its culture in academia in the United States and correct many misconceptions. One minor question: how do you see these murals compared to the 'Historia de Mexico' in the national palace?"

"Miguel, that is a very complicated question I'll leave to our dinner or even another time. I've got a "compromiso" [appointment] upstairs in ten minutes, so I'll see you Saturday."

I concluded that Rivera's "Historia de Mexico" in the national palace is much larger in scope, much more detailed, but the "germ" may have been at El Prado Hotel and the Education Ministry. The latter was overwhelming for both of us, Mexican schoolteachers and 'corrido' heroes and tales. And a whole new world and insight into the lives of the "pueblo" before and after the Revolution. Not sharing the Marxist worldview, I was still able to appreciate Rivera's, but remembered Agustín's much more balanced view of modern Mexico. Mariah shares my political views, but also was enthralled, especially with the role of women in the rural schools and literacy programs. More to come!

That was Tuesday. The rest of that week Mariah went regularly to the Ministry for meetings Graciela had set up, and it was a treasure trove. She met schoolteachers and administrators from primary, secondary and college levels, all women, who shared difficulties and triumphs in the

Mexican school system. She was taken on two occasions for school visits and for one, outside Mexico City on the way to Cuernavaca, I went with her. The results were heartening in most cases, but also sobering in others. Results would provide great material for her dissertation at Harvard. It became clear that Mexico has made great strides – more children in primary and secondary schools, more opportunity for trade schools or college, more books available and distance learning as well (national radio and educational TV). But, no surprise, there was a lack of funding in spite of the above. And still, a long-stereotyped notion, that women should either be at home or school teachers, and that "machismo" has not gone by the way in Mexico. Mariah was anxious to get Don Agustín's take on all this. That Saturday evening dinner opened us to yet another world.

13

AN EVENING WITH AGUSTÍN AND MICAELA YAÑEZ

We went in the Palafox's Mercedes with the chauffeur. Sr. Agustín lived in Coyoacán, in south Mexico City near the national university, the UNAM. It was a large, old house in a secluded part of the city, and that is hard to find in Mexico City. David said he had been there several times, for annual physicals, and a treatment or two, the idea being that the privacy of the Minister mattered a lot. The house was large, on two levels, with the ubiquitous stone wall in front with a "reja" or iron gate, and gardens on the other side. A doorman opened the gate, we were ushered to the "parking" and then inside. Although "informal," David said coat and tie were expected, and a nice evening dress for the ladies.

We were all greeted warmly by Agustín himself and his wife Micaela and then ushered into a very large "salón" or sitting – living room. I later noticed the décor was nationalistic - all Mexican. Paintings of scenes from Jalisco, the birthplace of both señor and señora Yañez, but to my great pleasure, an enlarged, framed photo of famous Mexican heroes Emiliano Zapata and PanchoVilla in the meeting of revolutionary leaders at the Presidential Palace on December 7, 1914. Other framed pictures were of President Benito Juárez and of the renowned José de Vasconcelos, first Secretary of the post – revolutionary Ministry of Education, then President of the National University and famous for his "La Raza Cósmica" and thesis of "mestizaje" [miscegenation] in Mexico. Vasconcelos was largely responsible in his regime for the national muralist movement of Rivera, Orozco and Siqueiros, all sponsored to depict Mexico and its Revolutionary principles in public art. All of this tied in to Agustín's later public life and decades of experience in the "preparatoria" schools in Jalisco (for young ladies, then young gentlemen and then the preparatory school for the University of Guadalajara), degree in Philosophy at the UNAM, governor of Jalisco and finally Secretary of Education.

I can't describe the feeling of being in that room surrounded by the essence of 20th century Mexican history. We were made to feel welcome by his wife Micaela, served drinks (your choice, imported whiskey, cerveza or wine, or coffee) and greeted warmly as if old friends. Wow. David and Agustín chatted of medical affairs, Micaela and Sarah of current goings – on in Mexico City, and Mariah and I just listened. But maybe twenty minutes later conversation turned to us, our research and Agustín saying again he was brought to reminiscing of the days of his youth by us. Dinner was early (for Mexico) at 7:00, scrumptious beef or seafood dishes, vanilla ice cream with the best chocolate sauce I had ever tasted, and strong, sweet demitasse "cafecitos" later. It was then Agustín invited us, as promised, into his large study – library for the real "dessert" – a viewing of the broadsides ["hojas volantes"] of José Guadalupe Posada, including at least two dozen of the famous "corridos."

My eyes got big when I actually saw the broadsides, old, yellowed in some cases, maintaining the rich colors in others, among them many "corridos." He had as well copies of the only photos known of Posada, in front of the "taller" or printing shop of Vanegas Arroyo in the old downtown, <u>circa</u> 1890. We saw: "hojas volantes" (single sheets); "cuadernillos" (chapbooks or booklets) of "Cancioneros" (popular songs); "Teatro Infantil" (Children's theater, puppets, marionettes); "Manuales" (Manuals in prose over writing love letters, cooking, medicine, home remedies, interpretation of dreams, Almanacs), and the main items: the "corridos" and "calatravas" [skeletons].

Señor Yañez surprised me then saying, "Miguel you are welcome to return to our house and use my library, but with stipulations I give to all: you can peruse and read all the broadsides and 'corridos,' take notes on all of them, take very limited pictures with flash, perhaps 5 to 10; none can leave this room or be xeroxed. I'm sorry but I cannot be here each time you come to study, but someone will be here, either Micaela or one of my secretaries. (He indeed relented later, giving me five precious original "hojas volantes" [broadsides]and five "corridos," saying "I know you will treasure them and take care of them. If sometime, you want to return them, no hurry, that will be fine too. Or better yet, place them in your famous library at Harvard, giving credit to your source, "your humble servant," and he smiled.

I digress to say what followed. Agustín also had "treasures" for Mariah, broadsides of the teachers in the countryside, government announcements and posters advertising the literacy campaigns and such. (She also was given permission for note taking and very limited photographs. For us the invitation was like being invited into a wing of the Library of Congress, or may I dare say, the Vatican Library).

So, what an evening! And what an example of the goodness and generosity of the Mexican intellectual and writer willing to share his lifetime collection and pride and joy with me and with Mariah. We all said goodbye without further conversation, a big, full day for both Agustín and David tomorrow, but also by setting up our visits and research for the balance of our days in Mexico City.

In the days that followed, almost two weeks, I took either a "pesero" or a bus on Insurgentes to Coyoacán and Agustín's house and library. Mariah came with me just once or twice but had her own affairs to manage: the interviews with the teachers, but in the Ministry of Education. She can probably get by on her own as well as or easier than I in huge Mexico City, so that was the plan.

14

MIKE'S RESEARCH

The essence of what I found during those two weeks and what I would take back to Harvard is as follows:

The cover illustrations and interior illustrations in the case of the chapbooks were done by Posada (1851 – 1913). Early on he did just a few woodcuts, but mainly did engraving on type metal (a lead alloy) using a "burin" to draw the lines. Later on, around 1900, he began to do relief etching on zinc, that is, drawing directly on a zinc plate with a special pen in greasy ink, then giving the plate an acid bath which would leave the lines he drew standing in relief. My research later in the library revealed that Posada's illustrations were of five major kinds:

1. The "calaveras" (skeletons made characters) based on pre – Columbian skulls and death goddesses and in part on the Spanish heritage of death orientation by monastic orders. In short, this is Mexico's lighthearted view of death for us all. The lady "Caterina" is most famous.
2. Disasters in Mexico and the use of "ejemplos" or moral examples as to why they took place.
3. National events: from Porfirio Díaz's days from 1876 to 1911 favoring the Oligarchy in Mexico, to Francisco Madero who defeated him in elections and then battle, he himself murdered

by General Huerta later. Then Emiliano Zapata and his call for agrarian reform from 1910 to 1917.

4. "Corridos" – the verse texts of songs and ballads meant to be sung by itinerant performers.

5. Adventures of Don Chepito Marihuano, a ludicrous middle-class bachelor (in skeleton - Calatrava form) and his social commentary.

6. Chapbook covers and illustrations of popular songs, theater, religious events, day to day events in Mexico.

These printed broadsides and chapbooks were sold throughout Mexico, as "street literature for the barely literate." One way was to the "papeleritos" or popular street vendors who stood on street corners singing or declaiming before a crowd. Religious broadsides were sold in the vestibules of churches. Vanegas Arroyo's (1850-1917) "Catalogue" was sent to all cities in the Republic (Agustín had several editions of this.)

Our host had samples of them all and pointed out some of the more famous: "Corrido da la Cucaracha," a broadside titled "Remate de Calaveras Alegres" featuring José Guadalupe Posada's famous female heroine - "La Catrina," "Gran Marcha Triunfal" featuring a victorious Francisco Madero, "El General Díaz Despide de la Nación" (en verso), "La Gran Calavera de Emiliano Zapata" (en verso), the broadside "Gaceta Callejera," (the anti-reelection campaign of Madero), "Corrido del Ataque a Puebla," "La Despedida del Revolucionario," "La Batalla entre los Federalistas y Zapatistas" and many more. There were many of the other types of broadsides: the role of Don Chepito, "Canciones Típicas" from 1894, stories of princesses and monsters, "Cartas Amorosas," (a guide to writing love letters), a hilarious, satirical broadside "Baile de los 41 Maricones," "Pleito de Suegras," The "Bicicleta," "Corrido de los Trenes," "La Mujer de 100 Maridos," Prayers to St. Anthony, (marriage saint for young ladies), in the end, a complete portrait of Mexican popular life and events, of the common people and of the rich and powerful.

Señor Yañez also had recordings of famous "corridos," among them "La Adelita," "Corrido de Chihuahua," "Zenaida," "Gabino Barrera," "La Valentina," "Corrido del General Francisco Villa," "Corrido de Benjamín Arguedo," and "Corrido de Benito Canales." After listening to a few, one could see the pattern of most: the introduction by the singer, the main story, and the obligatory "despedida" or goodbye.

Samples from some of the best known "corridos" are as follows:

"CORRIDO DE CHIHUAHUA"

Yo soy del mero Chihuahua
Del mineral de Parral
Y escuchen este corrido
Que alegre vengo a cantar. …

Ya me voy, ya me despido
No se les vaya a olvidar
Pa' gente buena Chihuahua
Que es noble, valiente y leal.

EL CORRIDO DE BENITO CANALES

Año de mil ochocientos
Es lo que digo yo,
Murió Benito Canales,
El gobierno lo mató. …

Y con ésta me despido
Debajo de los portales,
Estas son las mañanitas
De Don Benito Canales.

EL CORRIDO DE BENJAMÍN ARGUMEDO

Para empezar a cantar,
Para empezar a cantar,
Pido permiso primero
Señores son las mañanas
Señores son las mañanas
De Benjamín Argumedo…

Para empezar a cantar,
Para empezar a cantar
Pido permiso primero
Señores son las mañanas
Señores son las mañanas
Del General Argumedo

And not strictly following the permission – goodbye formula, but dealing with the two most famous women,

LA ADELITA

Si Adelita se fuera con otro
La seguiría por tierra o por mar
Si por mar en un buque de Guerra
Si por tierra en un tren militar.

VALENTINA

Una pasión me domina
Y es la que me hizo venir
Valentina, Valentina,
Yo te quisiera decir. …

Valentina, Valentina,
Rendido estoy a tus pies
Si me han de matar
Que me maten de una vez.

Needless to say, at the conclusion of the work I was asking myself, should this be the basis of the dissertation, perhaps not "The History of Abilene"? I'm thinking, for now, at least for the minor field, perhaps Mexican Literature and Popular Culture.

Oh, an aside, but important for the study in the literature classes back home: during one of the visits to the library, later on, I had the opportunity to talk to Don Agustín and bring up the subject of Brazil's "literatura popular em verso" or "A literatura de cordel" and say how close it seemed to be to the whole history of the broadsides and "corridos,' the verse, the songs and the illustrations. My knowledge of "cordel" was superficial to be sure, but I had seen enough of its "folhetos" or "romances" (corresponding to the 'hojas sueltas' and 'corridos' of Mexico) to tell Agustín of the amazing similarity in illustrations (but with woodcuts more than lithographs), the topics and the method of sale (compared to the "papeleritos" in Mexico). "Cordel" is stories in verse, "sung" or declaimed in the marketplace by the poet or vendor but it is not a ballad or song like the "corridos." National current events, history, politics, bandits, manuals for love letters, and satire on mothers – in – law are just a few of the shared topics, and "cordel" began and was popular at about the same time as the "corridos."

Agustín seemed pleased with the short message and we both agreed that it bring more attention by the scholars. He said, "Why not you? Do a comparative study and I'll see it gets published in Mexico." Whoa! A future Ph.D. waters at the mouth for possible publication of the dissertation and here it was as a gift! I agreed to keep him fully apprised but am thinking that with the emphasis on history and with Thomas Skidmore perhaps in charge, it would take some maneuvering on my part. Agustín had a ready reply: "What do you think historians base their histories on? It would be refreshing to see them get away from the dusty tomes in the national library and see what the campesinos and artisan class of Mexico really offer. And I can only assume, the same with Brazil. These two aspects of folk – popular culture surely fill the bill. Combine that with the 'muralistas' in Mexico and you my friend have a winner." My head was swimming with the possibilities.

15

CUERNAVACA AND RIVERA
- ACAPULCO REVISITED

Our time in Mexico was moving on, but not without one last jaunt, a Palafox – sponsored outing to the family condominium in Acapulco with the excuse of stopping in Cuernavaca on the way to see Cortes's palace and the last of Rivera's major murals. Don David wanted to provide us with a chauffeured van, two nights in the Palacio Hotel, one of his favorites in Mexico, and as many days in Acapulco as we wanted. The reader might recall Mariah and I did a wonderful jaunt to Acapulco for R and R our last time in Mexico, back in 1964, had a great time, and she loves the ocean, so we did it. But with one change, we traveled on the 5 Estrellas Autobus de Lujo [The 5 Star Luxury Greyhound – Style Coach]; we could be totally alone and private. David smiled, Sarah nodded and said nothing (uh oh, were we breaking her rules?), but Jaime and Lucas laughed and winked and just said, "Que se diviertan!" ["Have a good time!"] Like last time, we would return to Mexico City and spend a night or two with the family and tie up loose ends. David said, "At least allow me to treat you to the hotel in Cuernavaca; they owe me a favor or two for the medical conventions I've arranged there."

How could one argue? So the next morning we were dropped off at the Central Bus Station (you don't see many Mexicans arrive in a chauffeured

Mercedes) and were off for the short jaunt to Cuernavaca. "Land of Eternal Springtime" they say, and it *was* during our two day stay. A wonderful hotel was organized by Don David, the Palacio Hotel, of course named after Cortes's palace, was just outside of town, but with great gardens and on the slopes of Popocatépetl, so we did a hike part way up this famous volcano of the "Land of the Sleeping Giants." Then a swim in heated water in the pool and a candlelight dinner that night. Once again Mariah and Mike were experiencing wonderful tourism. We even went to a 16th century monastery close to the hotel, Dominican it was.

Tourism the next day was walking in that main plaza in town, but most of the day at the "Palacio de Cortés" and the murals, many a surprise to us. Now true veterans of Diego Rivera art, this was the same and yet different. It's a good story. The palace was supposedly a gift to Hernán Cortés for his role in the conquest of the Aztecs and Mexico. Construction was from the 1523 to 1528 and it looks the part – late medieval castle and fortress. Cortés visited but was much busier with landholdings in Morelos, "haciendas de caña de azúcar" [sugar cane plantations] and then his restlessness and foraging trips south to Chiapas and as far as Honduras of today. The title "Marqués del Valle de Oaxaca" was thus apropos. The family inherited the palace, used it some, but like the so many other cases of famous buildings of Mexican history, it was passed on to the government, played a bivouac role in the battle for Mexican Independence and the later war against the French, and finally was today a museum.

The murals are a "variation on a theme:" commissioned by the U.S. ambassador Dwight Morrow (of later fame, the father of Charles Lindbergh's wife and grandfather of their ill – fated son). Some controversy and mystery surrounds this: why a Marxist muralist sponsored by the USA? One theory is that Morrow owed President Calles a favor after he arranged for some investors from the U.S. But Rivera as usual insisted on a free rein on the topics. So, it's the same Spanish conquest of the natives, mistreatment for centuries, and finally the Revolution with hero Emiliano Zapata (of Morelos). However, the link to Morrow and future contracts to do murals in the U.S. got Marxist Rivera kicked out of the Communist Party in Mexico! Since I cannot reproduce the murals here (photo restrictions) I'll talk of three or four murals and illustrate the same topics from my own photos of times before in the stairway of the National Palace, "History of Mexico."

Pre – Columbian Mexico, Diego Rivera

First is the pre – conquest Indigenous Mexico with the usual idealized vision of the Aztecs and others, in this case Tajín (although Rivera showed a scene of Aztec sacrifice he would later link to Spanish cruelty afterwards).

Spanish Battle Aztecs, Diego Rivera

Then he depicts bloody battle scenes when the Spanish overcame the Aztecs in Tenochtitlán and others in Morelia.

Spanish Riches, Aztec Gold

A particularly telling mural is that of armor clad Spaniards, Cortés at their head with a secretary – scribe counting the gold they confiscated from the natives.

Tierra y Libertad, Diego Rivera

And finally, the depiction of Emiliano Zapata with his banner and main theme for his revolutionary activity in the upper center – "Tierra y

Libertad" - land and liberty – land reform for the landless peasants. He supported Madero, then lost faith in him and fought Madero's successors in the government until he was gunned down in an ambush on April 10, 1919.

After that long but worthwhile day with the murals (we were both a bit weary), we hopped the "5 Estrellas Autobus de Lujo" (the all night one coming from Mexico City) mainly because I wanted to relive the moment from my original trip in 1962, arriving to the sea at dawn. For readers who have seen "A Rural Odyssey II" from four years ago, it's a bit of "déjà vu" – coming over the hill from the dense rain forest of Morelos, looking through the palm trees and seeing the brilliant blue water of the Pacific. I hugged Mariah, said "We're home again," and we were, arriving at the less than luxurious downtown bus station, getting our bags, hailing a cab and then down the main avenue to Caleta – Caletillas beaches where the Palafox condominium was located. David had made the needed calls; the three person staff awaited us, carried the bags in, showed us to our separate rooms (did Sarah arrange this?), and then set out a wonderful breakfast – brunch for the overnight travelers. Because this was not our first time in Acapulco, we were patient enough and hungry enough to put off the beach until after the brunch and a nap. Freshly squeezed orange juice, papayas, bananas, grapes, then scrambled eggs with lots of bacon, fresh "bolillos" with that real Mexican butter and strawberry marmelade, any tiny chocolate cakes for dessert. And wonderful "café con leche."

We were both grubby from the all-night bus ride, so hopped into the shower, each helping each other to disrobe, and then one of those fun events. After drying each other off amidst some playful this and that, we hopped into the big king bed in the master suite (the staff had been clued in about the young lovers and their proclivities, leaving us to whatever young lovers do), made love and fell into a deep sleep.

Acapulco does this to you, puts time out of kelter. We woke up late afternoon, changed into beach attire and hit the beach. I had not actually seen Mariah in a bikini for some time, but if anything, she had improved with time – a slim figure but curves in all the right places. Me once again in that gringo boxer – style swimsuit. We grabbed beach mats, towels and some pesos for drinks and snacks and were soon in the cool, refreshing waves off Caleta. There were still two or three hours of late afternoon sun before the sunset, so it was perfect, no danger of a nasty Acapulco sunburn for the gringos.

That evening we dined in a wonderful outdoor restaurant on Caletilla, listened to a quiet trio that reminded me of the old time "Trío los Panchos" and began to wind down from the rather intense past three weeks in Mexico City and even Cuernavaca. There was close dancing after dinner, under the stars, and more intimate time back in the condo. Mariah requested we not talk "business" for at least a day or two, "plenty of time for that later," but we both agreed that it was indeed "mission accomplished." We watched some hilarious Mexican comedy show on the TV for an hour and both fell asleep again.

The next morning I awoke first, dressed in tourist walking shorts and polo shirt, and beach sandals, and took coffee out on the second-floor balcony of the condo. Héctor, the main man, provided me with the newspapers from the capital and even the latest "Time" magazine, and María the housekeeper arrived with wonderful café con leche, orange juice and "pan dulce." It was then I was able after considerable time to catch up on international events we had been avoiding the last three weeks. It was now mid – July and "Time" was full of frankly scary articles both on the national and international scenes. The "Space Race" was escalating, Viet Nam War protests spiraling almost out of control, Black protests since the Martin Luther King murder, the Viet Cong offensive at full speed, and basically most of America's youth no longer trusting their leaders. In Mexico the students were in solidarity, but most news was for the economic "stimulus" the Olympics would bring in October (yet to be seen by most).

Sleepyhead Mariah was up while I was reading, joined me now for breakfast, but was not ready for all the bad news. "Let it rest for now, please." I said, "Is this like being married?" She said, "Yes, except for the Mercedes ride, the condo on the beach, the waiters and housekeepers, breakfast appearing out of nowhere, and a full day in Acapulco ahead of us. Enjoy it 'Gringo Viejo.'" So, we did, that day and the next. We did get back to the topic of Mexico and why in the world we were there and went over all we had seen and accomplished the last three weeks.

Mariah first. She had firsthand reports on the Mexican Education System, literacy programs, television and radio instruction for the rural schools, and how they did counseling at the secondary level. This latter was way different than at home, mainly because college education was still only available to a tiny minority in Mexico, and your family's wealth or connections had most to do with getting to advanced learning (not that it wasn't somewhat the same at home, but we had far more resources, i.e. our own scholarships just an example). Recorded interviews from her own little tape recorder, piles of documents and reports jammed into one suitcase she bought just for that, and she was set to tackle courses in her third year in English – Counseling at Harvard come September. Best of all was the sure connection to resources of the Ministry with just a letter (that would be read and answered) or a call to Minister Yañez.

In my case I had an amazing trove of information – hand written notes on what I had read, newspaper accounts, photos and historic documents (due to Agustín's generosity) on the entire gamut of the broadsides and "corridos" from Vanegas Arroyo's and Guadalupe Posada's popular press, plus now a complete picture of the ideology and practice of the Post – Revolutionary Government's policy of public art promoting the ideals of Mexico. Where this all would lead I was not sure, but would definitely discuss it as a topic for the dissertation, or at least for a minor field.

We concluded the short stay in Acapulco, two more leisurely days at the beach, making it up to the cliff divers' domain one more time and enjoying a spectacular sunset over the Pacific, and then a rainy drive the next morning to the bus station and a downpour via 5 Estrellas back to Mexico City. We took a taxi to the apartment and immediately called Don

David and discussed plans for our last two days in the city: to wit, packing up the apartment the next day, spending the final night at the Palafox residence with a "despedida" dinner once again at the sky – high Torre Latino Americana restaurant with all the family.

16

A "GOODBYE DINNER" –
FUN AND FANTASY

That night was also a bit of a reprise of a similar goodbye dinner back in 1964. Dressed for fine dining, Mariah, I, Dr. David, Sarah, Jaime and fiancée Raquel, and brother Lucas were all there. Champagne flowed and then fine wine with dinner and the wonderful "cafecitos" later. Food was your choice – seafood or Mexican style "bistec con arroz valenciano" or the Mexican "comida típica" plate. Dr. David wanted to know first of all how the accommodations in Cuernavaca and Acapulco turned out – "Excelente en todo sentido," Mariah quickly answered. We filled them in on the newest batch of Rivera murals we saw in Cuernavaca, but talked more about how beautiful the beach, waves and ocean at Acapulco were.

"From your smiles and demeanor, I think it all agreed with you," Jaime said, a bit of a smirk on his face. (And a knee nudged under the table by Raquel, a sign to "cool it.") Mariah looked at me, smiled again, and blushed a bit. Conversation turned to the wedding preparations coming for just a few months later for Raquel and Jaime. She said, "Mariah and Miguel, you may not be that familiar with such affairs in Mexico, just look at the society page on Sunday morning in 'Excelsior,' but it all gets a bit complicated. Although Jaime and I are not exactly even Reform Jewish in our beliefs, there are customs we shall follow, like the open-air ceremony with the canopy, the breaking of the champagne glass, the food and lots of dancing. Enough of that as we move along, but maybe you can fly down for that weekend (she looked over at Dr. David with an inquisitive look)." He nodded and smiled, the look of just leave it to me. We just said we would see, but it would be at the top of the priority list if at all possible.

Talk went on about all the construction, traffic jams, general chaos of D.F. getting ready for the Olympics in October. The Azteca Soccer Stadium and "Estadio Olímpico Mexicano" in the UNAM area were the main large sites, but smaller venues were being prepared all over the city with even Insurgentes Theater used for wrestling, and sailing at Acapulco. And they built a huge "Olympic Village" to house all the athletes. Much was behind schedule in July but the Palafoxes were not worried, "Mañana you know," said Dr. David.

We talked some about the chaotic, worrisome world situation, mainly the Viet Nam War, the demonstrations, the assassinations, and Mexico's incipient unrest, student solidarity with U.S. students. I said that we were really out of the loop on most recent happenings but reiterated that both Mariah and I had other priorities – a final third year of classes for our Ph.D. programs, comprehensive exams to come, and of course dissertations. And I added we both had a big boost in that area from this stay in Mexico. Mariah seconded all that with some detail on her findings and hopes. Dinner concluded with happy toasts and best wishes for mutual good fortune.

The next day we were busy organizing all the research materials, packing them up and getting ready for the next morning's flight to Kansas City. Dinner that night was at the Palafoxes, talk once again of all we had learned in the research, expressing gratitude to Dr. David and Sarah, Jaime and Lucas. We told of the plan to go to Overland Park and see Benjamin and Ariel, and of course all the Mexico Palafoxes sent their best. Once again there was talk of a reunion for all at the wedding in Mexico City later in the year. The more they talked, the more Mariah and I thought it would be a great idea, and we assured all we would convince

Benjamin and Ariel to come as well. The night ended with cordials before the fireplace and, you might have guessed, another 'concert" by the 'gringo guitarist. I did not know one new song since last time, but no one remembered anyway and there was great enthusiasm. Then off to bed (separate bedrooms), up early the next morning, a final terrific breakfast and then David and Sarah accompanying us in the Mercedes to the airport. Sad, teary goodbyes, and then after just a one hour delay, on Mexicana to Kansas City.

17

VISITS TO THE RELATIVES ONCE AGAIN

Benjamin and Ariel met us at the Kansas City airport, and we drove to the house right away. They were relieved we were safe and were full of questions about Mexico and the relatives. Over dinner that night, we basically filled them in on all the reader already knows. Everyone agreed that Jaime and Raquel's wedding before Hanukkah might be a possibility. And we got their take on all the recent events at home in the U.S., Dr. Benjamin a bit wary of what might be coming. The next day it was a return to our favorite spot on the Plaza and you guessed it, the Deli for pastrami sandwiches, cheesecake and a cold beer (we did not have any of the Deli food in Mexico). The rest of the day it was just quiet time at home and getting ready for the sojourn out to Abilene.

It was only on the drive on the Interstate home that we talked a bit of what our plans and options might be for the coming year – the intense fall semester finishing courses, preparation for comprehensive exams, and spring term and summer of research and writing of the dissertations. A huge order! We would get back to our respective housing on campus by mid – August and have almost a full month to tidy up Mexico work and plan for a very intensive year. We were now in late July and early August, so the summer weather was lousy – hot, humid, and windy. Welcome to

Kansas. We had made a reservation at the motel north of town near the Interstate, so checked in and then called Mom and Dad. Mom quickly invited us for dinner that night, saying Caitlin would help with the cooking for the "reunion," fried chicken, potatoes and gravy, and green beans. What else?

Mom and Dad were much the same, albeit, older, moving a bit slower, but the same in spirit. Mom gave me and Mariah a big hug, and even Dad did the same; we just had about twenty minutes before Caitlin and Ron would arrive so we would have to repeat any news for them. It had been a very hot summer, but with two or three good rains, so after a good wheat crop and alfalfa it looked like corn might be as good as well. More on all that from Ron. The vegetable garden was now pretty depleted by the summer heat, but Mom's flowers at home were spectacular, and the little shed out back was full of black walnuts to be shelled that fall for fudge, cookies and homemade walnut bread. I kidded Mom saying she would have to send us a "care" package, and she was ready to do it. "Naah. It would get beat up in the mail or melt. Thanks anyway."

Once everyone got there, incidentally Caitlin and Ron leaving the four kids at home with a babysitter but with our promise to come out the next day or two, we all sat down for drinks (Dad pulled out his Old Grand Dad pint bottle, a two or three time a year occurrence, but Caitlin brought a nice wine and Ron a six pack of Coors beer, neither a mainstay at the O'Brien's house). Ron, not one to either mince words or avoid a joke, said, "You two still not hitched? How in the hell long has it been anyway Mike? Folks around here have about given up on you two." Mom was a bit embarrassed, and Mariah blushed, but I just said, "Same ole,' same ole' Ron. We are in love, but plans are on hold until we both get the degree from school, so don't quite hold your breath yet." That seemed to squelch that particular topic.

The next two hours were just spent getting caught up, the farm scene, the town and county news (marriages, divorces, deaths), and our retelling the news from Mexico. The research really meant little to the Abilene crowd so we glossed over that, but told of Mariah's family, the tourist sites in Mexico City, Cuernavaca and Acapulco. Mom had still never seen the ocean so we tried to describe that. I promised to send photos as soon as we could get all our film developed and copies made. Mariah's research meant more to Mom, the former country one – room schoolhouse teacher out on the eastern Colorado plains, and I think Mariah tried to make it all as familiar as possible to her. Caitlin had taught as well before she and Ron got married, so it was indeed a family of teachers and farmers. They all wanted to know the plan for the next year so we explained as best we could, saying nothing definite would be known until next Spring, that is, in 1969. The food was great and Mariah, Mom and Caitlin were chattering away in the kitchen after supper while Dad, Ron and I talked in the living room, mainly about the farm and general farm developments around the country. In spite of the good weather, the good summer crops and maybe a bumper corn crop on the way, times over all were not good for farming – low prices for crops, sky – rocketing machinery costs, and many farmers not able to make the mortgage payments. Like I've said before, Ron and Stan were okay because they had a large amount of acreage and a diversified operation, crops and cattle.

We would just spend two or three more days in town but try to get around to the usual places, St. Andrew's, the 3rd street tavern for gossip from Wally Gallatin, and a visit with Dr. Halderson up at the college. As far as relatives knew, the college was really catching on in Central Kansas, offering an option to Abilene and local kids who would not make it to the big three in Lawrence, Manhattan or Emporia. The shock would come with that conversation.

Dr. Halderson was gracious as ever, delighted to see us, and full of ideas (he had obviously begun thinking and planning in regard to us). After we told of our recent trip for research in Mexico and the plans for this next year, he had a lot to say. "This is all extremely ambitious. I hope you can carry it off. I have something for you to think about. Our college is doing very well, is considered a fine, four – year small college, and we are considering launching our first Master's Programs. I'd like you to consider an offer I've been thinking about since you both flew the coop here for Harvard; if you both have Ph.Ds. after next summer, I/we at the college would like to persuade you to return to Abilene and your posts here at the college. Mariah, you would be an Assistant Professor of English with tenure, and in addition a new post, Dean of Women, with major counseling duties. Mike, you would be an Assistant Professor with tenure with equal appointments in History and Spanish. Salaries would be commensurate with your degrees (and Harvard boosts that) at $40,000 each. This is a very generous even hefty offer, but we know your work record and with these new qualifications, we want to get our foot in the door before other offers come. We are sure you will be in demand. We would utilize both of you as well for recruiting for DDE College throughout the State of Kansas to boost our own enrollment. I cannot understate the value of the Harvard pedigree for us. You know I always wanted you back, so please consider seriously this offer."

I looked at Mariah, and I think we were both taken aback by that offer. "How soon would you need to know, Dr. Halderson?"

"You are familiar with normal college routine, recruiting and the like, so the sooner the better, but I would say at least by March of next year. If I am correct you will have coursework and exams done by then and be well along with the dissertations."

Mariah spoke for both of us: "Please let us think about this for a while; we can assure you we will give it serious consideration. I think that you have a special case for a small, public four – year college – the Eisenhower Name – so that does carry unusual weight. How about an update in September from Boston and we can either proceed or not from there, Mike, do you agree?"

I said I did, we asked a few more questions about the plan, received some clarification, and thanked the good Dr. and were on our way. Out in the car we both looked at each other, smiled and maybe even laughed a bit, both amazed but agreeing that our decisions so far were indeed good ones. Our first job offer!

There was little to report on the rest of Abilene before we drove back to the city, spent one night with Benjamin and Ariel and then flew back to Boston. On the plane we exchanged ideas and opinion about the next nine months, what might be ahead of us, but I've got the cart before the horse. School first.

18

TRIALS AND TRIBULATIONS – GETTING THE DEGREES

It sounded difficult. It was worse than that. They say "ambition knows no bounds;" somebody smarter than us said that. I wrote a while back that I was in an accelerated Ph.D. program at Brown in Fall, 1966, and that did not change at Harvard. Mariah's Ph.D. program turned out to be accelerated but because she already had a Master's in English before she started in Law School at Harvard in 1966. I'm not complaining (well, I am); it was our decision. To put it all in a nutshell (appropriate word, nut), here's the picture; I'll fill in the gaps as we go.

In the Fall of 1968, I did three courses and began the cramming for the Ph.D. comprehensive exams for February, 1969. The excruciating organizing and writing the dissertation would follow from March to early August when I finished what Thomas Skidmore said was "a rather small opus but to the point. You may have set a record for brevity for Harvard." He added later after a few beers in a local bar, "I hope your lectures are that short, but, hey, don't forget to always throw in a laugh or two. What do Kansans laugh at anyway? The city slicker and the cow pie? Maybe that old Indian story when the Easterner driving to the Grand Canyon across those boring endless miles of Kansas saw a brave on his pony and his squaw lady walking behind. 'Hey, brave, why is your squaw walking?' 'She got no pony.' Just kidding, soon to be *Dr. O'Brien*, just kidding."

Mariah did three courses and then the same idiotic routine as I, also doing comps in February. She's a lot smarter than I am, and a better writer, so she had less trouble with the dissertation and actually had the whole typed manuscript in one of those Xerox paper boxes by mid – July 1969. That's the short of it.

I suppose we could have quit, kaput, the whole shebang. Some did. Massive national protests followed the Democratic National Convention in August. The background was that peace talks with North Viet Nam were understandably going nowhere because the U.S. would not agree to stop bombing of the north. Hubert Humphry who said he would honor LBJ's politics beat out Eugene McCarthy, the anti- Viet Nam War candidate. Protests outside the park culminated in the arrest and trial of the "Chicago 8" and a long process of conviction and then acquittal. October brought good and bad: 24,000 U.S. troops were required to return to Viet Nam for a *second* tour of duty.

Closer to "home" for Mariah and me was the real tragedy of the "Tlateloco Massacre" in Mexico City on October 2, 1968. Massive student protests against the oppressive regime of Díaz Ordaz were countered by police and military firing real bullets in the Plaza de las 3 Culturas with deaths not only of students but innocent bystanders. Closer to home we all saw on the TV the U.S. black athletes' 'black power' protest after winning races in the Olympics in Mexico City.

The only good news was the Apollo Space program with manned flights around the earth and then the moon. And good or bad news, depending on your point of view, Richard Nixon was elected President in November 1968.

All this was going on during that hectic and intense Fall for us at Harvard. There was one hiatus, but it involved just three days - a very quick weekend for Jaime and Rachel's wedding in Mexico City in late December but before Christmas. Just a few words about that. We flew to

Kansas City on a Saturday morning, joined Dr. Benjamin and Ariel and got an afternoon flight to Mexico City. We were honored to stay at the Palafox home, but fully enjoyed all the wedding festivities the next day. Lucas and of course Jaime were not there on Saturday night after Shabbat had ended but were off for the Mexican version of a bachelor party. Lucas told me later it was not the raucous debauchery associated with the same back home in the U.S. It was hosted by Jaime's best friend, an associate of the company, at his home. Twenty good buddies had toasts to the groom, told a few stories, and did traditional blessings. The outdoor ceremony with the traditional canopy and large reception dinner and dancing was in the large garden of the De León mansion in Lomas. The bride and groom would do their honeymoon at the ocean in Bora Bora. I was at a loss for understanding all that was going on, but Mariah explained as things happened. The best part was the truly joyful reunion of Benjamin with his brother David, and Ariel with Sarah, and Mariah with her cousins. Jaime and Rachel I think made a special effort to thank us all, both saying they would be waiting for news of the same for Mariah and me. That remained to be seen. "Later," we said. After a sad goodbye we all flew back to Kansas City and Overland Park the next day on Monday.

We did not even go to Kansas City or Abilene at Christmas because of study and let's call it was it was, *cramming* for comprehensive exams that came the following February. For me there would be three areas: the minor in matters of Portugal and Brazilian Literature, the minor in Spanish American Literature, mainly the novels of the 20th century, and the major in Latin American History with emphasis on the U.S. Southwest and Mexico. Each day was eight hours of essay writing, but I thought I really did well, mainly because my heart was in it. Mariah's were just as tough, her three days with the first the minor in Counseling, another in Shakespeare (query: can one minor in old Will's work?) and American Literature, emphasis on 20th century prose, Faulkner, O'Connor and Roth the biggies. We were not really that worried about passing; they don't invest three years in you to flunk you, but it was not pro – forma either. As we would both say and agree months later, it was kind of like the old country song, "I've forgotten more than you'll ever know about … ." There was a one-week break, seriously suggested by respective advisors and then intense work on the dissertations.

In that interim and weeks that followed in Spring of 1969 there was mostly bad news, but the U.S. and North Viet Nam did start peace talks in January. But further actions put the kibosh to that, to wit, the reporting of U.S. forces killing old men, women and children in the village of Than Phong in Viet Nam. On a minor level, bad news for me - the old baseball player Mickey Mantle, the hero of my youth, was finally retiring from the Yankees in March, sad, but long overdue. I used to check the Kansas City Times every morning on the farm in Abilene to see the box score and if he hit a home run. And our real Abilene hero, General Dwight D. Eisenhower died at his farm in Gettysburg the same month.

The continuing saga of Black Power boiled over in protests at no less than Duke University and then Cornell, in April, followed by martial law on the campus at Berkeley for the same reason.

I had other things on my mind, a kind of tunnel vision it is true, but a priority: the dissertation. I jumped the gun earlier in this narration; here are more details. Regarding the dissertation, on my part there was a bit of a thorny discussion with Dr. Skidmore. He quite frankly thought there was not enough new material for my "History of Abilene" for one thing, and he did not see an intellectually strong link to my major of Latin American History. "Leave Abilene for an article or maybe a book if you learn a lot more of the era and the area." We both agreed that tying in the research from Mexico the previous summer was the ticket, "if you do it right." History, most people agree, is written by the winners, and in Mexico it was the PRI and the Constitution of 1917 that were the driving forces behind the last fifty years. The entire economic, social, political, and religious reality that the Revolution fought for and embraced to change was depicted on at least three levels: the major and minor events of the years of the Revolution, the depiction in Mexican Literature in the "Novels of the Revolution," but uniquely in this case: the popular culture of the street literature of Posada's broadsides and the ballads of the "corridos" and the arts "in between the lines," above all, public art of the "muralistas" in propagandizing the government programs.

"There are your three major chapters; do an introduction to Porfirio Diaz's Mexico and what he inherited and a conclusion on what the PRI put into practice and you my friend will have a book that Harvard University Press will be glad to look at."

I won't even try to say much about Mariah's dissertation, but just that it involved tying the threads of 20th century American Prose together. Like I say, she kept her nose to the grindstone and had it finished in July.

What I have not said is that back in March after we had passed exams and were started on the dissertations, we had a very long talk and made the decision to take up Dr. Halderson's offer and return to Kansas and Abilene, at least for the foreseeable future. The whys and wherefores are important. For me it was clearer, a return "home" to do what I loved, teaching and research (the nebulous but promising "History of Abilene,") plus be with my family and the Kansas old reality. For Mariah, what finally tipped the scales were the memories of just how much she had done and shared with the students at the Juco, especially her mentoring of the young girls, and how that influence now could be greater as Dean of Women. Proximity to Overland Park played a role, but lesser, after all, now in the jet age travel home could be done from anywhere. And she had important things to share of America in its literary heritage.

Should I leave this for later? I formally proposed to Mariah that March, she accepted, and we decided to make plans once we had settled in our new lives in Abilene that Fall of 1969. The engagement ring was small, modest, but did bring tears to my now betrothed partner. It was not as though we had not been talking about it for, let's see, for three years, but we had always said, "after we get our degrees." We both had always said we wanted our freedom, but a Jewish Rabbi told Mariah the real freedom is when you do marry. Hmm.

At the height of our writing and difficulties with dissertation advisers, outside the library windows and the tiny, soot covered windows of our rooms where we wrote, reality went on: the first U.S. troops began withdrawal from Viet Nam in July. And Teddy Kennedy, the only one left of my Kennedy heroes, in effect "blew it" with the drunken night in New England and driving his car into the Chappaquiddick River and leaving Mary Jo Kopeke to drown. You could literally hear the air go out of the high flying balloon of the entire Kennedy legacy, and what remained of the Democratic party's good days fizzle like a Bronx cheer. Then a bright note came – Neil Armstrong and his two brave cohorts on the Moon, and for just a little while it felt good to be an American, in fact proud. I guess feeling good was more for some than others when the flower children, dope, rock n' roll, and promiscuity blended in with war protests in August at Woodstock.

Those were the exact days when our dissertations were approved and respective graduations postponed until the following January. We said our goodbyes to Boston and the East, including emotional goodbyes to mentors and professors who all wished us well out on "the frontier," but me sensing they did not think this was a wise decision. Clothes, books, favorite records, an old guitar and memories – all piled into the Chevy and heading home.

PART II

1

YOU CAN GO BACK
HOME AGAIN

Those three long days of driving were filled with time gazing out the
car windows, both of us wondering about the future, but also reminiscing
about the last three years, all we had done and seen, and best of all,
accomplished! We were proud of each other, but at the same time, a bit
fearful and cautious about what lay ahead. But also we were in love, and
like the late corn we saw in the fields, now tasseled out and soon to be
harvested, we wondered if our own future like the harvest would be so
bountiful. There was much to share with family and lots of hard work and
an as yet unfulfilled dream ahead.

The first "homecoming" was of course in Overland Park, joyful, and
with Benjamin and Ariel bursting with happiness and contentment for
their only daughter, and proud as well for her "goy" and future husband.
There was a happy dinner that evening with bottles of champagne and
talk of things to come, not in small part, the wedding surely not far
off. Ben said, "We knew that nothing would stop you two from those
academic challenges and dreams, and Ariel and I both have talked so
many times of how good you are for each other. Shalom." Mariah took
her mom and dad's respective arms and said, "Hey you two, he's a *good*
man, a real mensch, and we deeply love each other. Everything will be all

right." I don't know if they needed reassuring, but those words certainly accomplished it, and I confess, for me too, farm boy, Irish and Catholic by upbringing, in a whole new world. The same could of course be said for Mariah when we arrived in Abilene and went immediately to see Mom and Dad.

The House, Abilene

It was mid – afternoon with the proviso we would spend the night and be out early the next a.m. for apartment hunting. We had called from Overland Park to give them a warning! The same joy as in Kansas City was in the air. When Mom saw that engagement ring, she laughed, saying, "I have been waiting so long for this I've forgotten how long it has actually been. Mariah, Sean and I knew from the first time we met you that you indeed are perfect for our son. I will admit that your being Jewish although not exactly a problem, was an unknown. Why didn't he bring you to mass? That was the question. Ha Ha. We just didn't really know anything about all that. But the important thing is you two love each other, are committed to each other. I am sure you have the religious aspect worked out. And we are so proud of you sticking to your guns for the advanced degrees. And we are even happier that you are back home at DDEC. Whoops, I've said enough."

Mariah gave her a big hug and so did I and then it was Dad's turn. He smiled and sat down in that big easy chair in the living room saying, "I'll just listen." Caitlin and Ron were coming over after he fed the cattle and she arranged a babysitter for just a couple of hours; supper would be about 6 p.m., Mom saying would you mind if it's such chile and salad tonight? We assured her it's no problem and we could make a run to Zoll's west side store (not really, but to the westside liquor store for two bottles of cold champagne and to the Dairy Queen for a frozen ice cream pie). Sure enough, Caitlin and Ron arrived about two hours later, giving us time to partially unload the car and settle in upstairs for the night.

There were more hugs when Caitlin spied the engagement ring and immediately gave Mariah and me a hug and Ron let out a big whoop wondering when we would actually make it all "legal" (with a laugh). We weren't that certain at that point but said within the next year. We opened the champagne, had Mom's chile and the DQ ice cream cake, and then the rest of the evening was catching up on local news, mostly farm news and the recent fair and rodeo (we had just missed it, one of my favorites growing up), and our telling what the "grind" had been like back in Boston for the last few months. "But getting it all done will make the jobs here so much easier, and we can really concentrate on the new tasks at hand. I would not have told you before, but most people who try to work full time and do a dissertation as well end up a bundle of nerves! We do not know a whole lot about routine at the college, but I am sure some will be like before and some different. Mariah mainly, with that 'high – falutin' title' of hers plus normal teaching (I poked her in the ribs and laughed; fortunately, so did she). We are exhausted and beat up from it all, so if you do not mind, we'll make it an early evening. We can catch up more in just a couple of days (that was firmed up with Ron and Caitlin's invitation for Sunday dinner at the farm, and a chance to meet the kids once again, and Mom and Dad always pleased to see the grandchildren). We were out like lights up in the tiny middle bedroom upstairs, but no matter.

Next morning we were both up early, Dad already in the kitchen doing his bacon and eggs, Mom resting in a bit. It gave us a chance to talk about the farm, the horses and to kind of see how he was doing. Thank God he was much the same, a few aches and pains, but perking right along. I left Mariah to join him at the breakfast nook and gave my old landlady Mrs. Stevens a call about apartment availability. She said, "I saved the nicest for you two, just in case. Everyone in town knew you were coming home. In fact, you are a bit of celebrities for us. Come whenever you want and take a look at it." Fine.

We decided to go later that morning and then check in up at school with Dr. Halderson. Engaged and that being enough to satisfy society's norms for us, we ended up renting Mrs. Stevens' apartment, a two-bedroom place once again on North Buckeye in one of the old Victorians where I had a single apartment back in 1964 - 1966. The big difference is we were now "roommates" to say the least and prepared to handle whatever the local "gossips" might pass around town on those old party telephone lines. We did not consider Mariah's old place mainly because nothing large enough was available there. And once again, if need be, we could walk to the college for exercise, fresh air, or auto emergency. We did however not do a one year's lease, but month to month, more expensive but flexible for come what may. Thinking about that, we did not know what the next summer in 1970 would bring.

That afternoon marked the return to now DDEC (Dwight D. Eisenhower College), a welcome back meeting with Dr. Halderson, settling into our new offices (more spacious for Mariah with her administrative duty as well). *This* is the culmination of what had started as a long-range plan three years ago back in 1966, and in our minds was just the first of what we hoped would be a promising post – doc career. His secretary, Griselda, greeted us warmly and even gave Mariah a hug, saying how much *everyone* from the "old days" was glad we were back. She ushered us into his office and he with a huge smile said, "Welcome home. I planned and even prayed you two would be here with us again. I can't thank you enough for considering this small college in Abilene after Brown and Harvard. I and others will do our utmost to help you in making it the right decision." We both reiterated why we had decided to return to Abilene, what the reader already knows, emphasizing it was the wonderful teaching experience, camaraderie of DDEC colleagues, and local friendships that weighed heavily in the decision. Plus, of course, Dr. Halderson's faith in us and the generous salary offer.

"Classes start in ten days so let's get right at it. Mike, you will be an Assistant Professor with tenure (a very unusual but satisfying decision on our part); we expect you will be dividing your time between History and Spanish, probably a 2 to 1 classroom schedule, with appropriate advising duties. There, by the way, is a whole new international component, very small but important; we'll talk of that later. Mariah, you will have the same rank and status, once again very unusual the rank *with* tenure. But you both proved your worth for three years and we are confident you will only advance and mature now. Mariah, we anticipate you will do two upper – division courses in English, or however you choose, and what amounts for now to one – third time administration as our new Dean of Women. Professor Stavros who has done yeoman work ever since the DDE Juco was founded is ready to retire and "travel to see the world." At this point one – third time should be about right with duties commensurate, mainly counseling of academic affairs and in a few instances, personal guidance for our young ladies. We all recall the terrific work you did with the same type of students for three years. We also remember from three years ago the fine work you both did in recruiting, and I have some ideas for that as well, but we can have that conversation in just a few weeks. By the way, although you are not *new* faculty, but old friends returning, the first Friday p.m. after classes we all have to stay on campus for what I would call a "welcome back party," a "command performance" as it were.

The Rose Window, St. Andrews

The next Sunday we joined Mom and Dad for mass at St. Andrew's and said a happy hello to Father Kramden afterwards; he drew me aside saying, "Please call me soon, I think I can help you and Mariah with the 'religious thing' (surmising he knew all about Irish Catholic – Jewish situations). We would eventually do that. The Zimmermans came up, high school buddy Luke's parents and his brother Grady and wife, said hello and welcome back, as did Stan and his wife and a few of the old faces I grew up with. Mariah knew all these people and I think she felt almost as much at home as I. We promised Mom and Dad we would see them later at Caitlin's for a Sunday afternoon dinner, and we would get to see the kids.

Then we decided to do a drive around town and snapped a few photos.

Dwight D. Eisenhower

The Lebold Mansion

Mariah and I had a big breakfast at the new café up near the Interstate and I suggested that drive around town and maybe out in the country around town, then a short nap before Ron and Caitlin's. It was fun and didn't take long to do the "circuit," south of town out by Brown's Park and the Power and Light Station, a quick run into the Eisenhower Center parking lot, noting the reconstructed west wall of the Museum, the new modern Chapel and the Library to the south. I did the circle around town: out west south of the Santa Fe tracks, over the tracks and by the big old flour mill and grain elevator, out southwest of town by the tiny airport and the beautiful river bottom farms (relatives or friends of Ron and Stan's).

Then it was out old Highway 40 past the Greyhound Racing Course, the drive-in movie theater which I told a few stories about and had even taken Mariah back during our first year in town in 1963 - 1964, back into town and all around the fairgrounds, the old 4-H fair barns, the National Guard building where we used to have dances, and the CCC stone stadium where all the summer baseball took place, with the rodeo grounds around it, now much modernized with new ball fields for the kids. Then the bandshell which brought back so many memories, from the Thursday night band concerts in the summer and music with Jeremiah and Loren from high school days, and finally to the swimming pool with all its memories. Mariah had already heard all my stories, and when she began yawning, I took a hint and we headed to our new "home" for a one – hour nap before the trek out to the farm. We would leave the rest maybe for the following Sunday. We had that welcome nap, both still I think winding down from Boston and the cross-country drive and left for Caitlin's at 3 p.m., both of us saying it would be an early night because, guess what, first day at school would be on Monday.

The New Farm House

The big change, and it was that, the old farmhouse where I grew up was gone. Ron and Stan had built a beautiful red brick ranch style home; it was a large one floor. They were starting it when we had headed back east to school; it was finished a year ago, but I guess I have not had occasion to say much about it. But after a short tour (not that day but a couple of weeks later), I could see it was not all that was changed. You might say, and it was unintentional, and I guess inevitable, Dad's old place was almost unrecognizable. We did not talk about that until later that Fall when Mariah and I were in the living room in town and I brought it up. It would come into play along with all the other changes we would eventually see on farms around town and in the county.

It was a bit of bedlam, the kids came running out, yelling and shouting, all saying "Uncle Mike and Aunt Mariah, welcome home!" Mariah glanced over at me, I just shrugged my shoulders and said, "How does it feel? You may see these kids up at the college if we hang around here long enough! Ha ha." I could tell she was not close to being ready to think about that. The kids all wanted to show us their rooms (boys' and girls'), toy guns and model airplanes with the boys, dolls and writing projects and clothes from the girls. Times had changed, but times had not changed. Instead of a Roy Rogers' gun belt and pistol, it was Marshall Dillon's from "Gunsmoke," but the BB guns were the same, the old Red Ryder model based on the "Winchester 73" with its pump handle. Mariah had to ooh and aah at the new school dresses and shoes, and we both were told we would have to see the 4-H projects. Caitlin rescued us, sending the kids into the big basement playroom with the color TV, and the adults had a chance to talk over drinks upstairs in the big living room. I noted Caitlin had a large piano in what she called "the music room," and we all laughed and recalled music room days from the old farmhouse growing up.

They all wanted to know the latest from DDEC and more of our last year in Boston and the travels to Mexico (maybe curious of Mariah's family and relatives). I raved about Mariah's parents, brother, and aunt and uncle and cousins in Mexico City; she recounted our travels emphasizing Acapulco (farm landlubbers in Kansas loved that). Neither of us detailed the research, topics rather unfamiliar or even uninteresting in Abilene, but did tell once again (we had said this before in short previous visits) of the skyscrapers of New York, the colonial history of Boston, and those mansions in Newport. They all were most curious as to duties at DDEC (that name stuck in Abilene and surroundings and was becoming famous in its own way). Caitlin was very attuned to Mariah's duties as she had some of the same for years, albeit never on the college level or Dean of Women; she wondered about that. Ron just said Abilene was really happy to have a four-year school and it added a lot to the community, but he and brother Stan, both graduates of K – State in Manhattan would get their football "fix" there come fall. He invited us to join them for a long Saturday later on, saying as much as they donate to the college, he surely could get some good tickets.

2

"BACK IN THE SADDLE AGAIN"

Monday came soon enough with the usual mass confusion of late enrollment, finding classrooms, new classes, new students first time on campus and for that matter, "new" faculty. My schedule was basically like before - Spanish 101 and 201 in the morning, 9:40 and 10:40 five days a week, U.S. History of the Southwest at 12:40 after an hour's break on MWF. That left time in the afternoon for office hours and the old nemesis, faculty meetings. I intentionally left Friday p.m. free for maybe an early get a way once in a while. And there evolved a pizza and beer one - hour get together at the new Giuseppe's up on north Buckeye near the interstate. Mariah with her Spanish and French joined us sometimes, duties permitting. Ah, things for Mariah were much the same, two English classes in the a.m. MWF but with all day T and TH and Friday a.m. for the counseling duties. We were both reintroduced that first Friday p.m. to all faculty, coffee, tea and cookies you know, but a warm welcome by former colleagues. As time goes on, I'll tell of those we had enough in common with to socialize with in town, the "normal" connections due to interests and age.

There was one new duty for me (as promised by Dr. Halderson) – International Student Advisor. It did not involve so much as to curriculum since the students would meet with respective faculty in their majors but was more just a "friendly liaison" to check on them and see how they were doing not only in a different country, but in Kansas, no small order! And honestly, there were not many. DDEC was up to 1000 enrollment, quite a jump from our days of 1963, and there were about thirty students from outside the U.S. One might wonder why? The plains of Kansas? A new four-year public college? One word: EISENHOWER. The reader may have no idea what that magic word and name meant both inside and outside our country. Ike was still the tactical genius of Allied Commander in WW II, the former president (albeit perhaps for publicity) of no less than Columbia University in New York, and respected former President of the nation. He had just died in 1968, but the memories were still fresh. The thirty students were primarily from Spanish America – Mexico by far the most – but ten from around Europe (where Eisenhower was still so highly revered) from England, France, and Spain. I received help from Mademoiselle Cheri Massenet from the French section and our colleague – representative from Spain, Simón Rodríguez from Salamanca, on an as needed basis. Parties were to come!

Mariah's classes and duties would slowly evolve, much more about that as they happened, but testing both her resolve and her talents. I think the reader can see that we were not exactly looking for something to fill our time; routine took care of that and at times it became a bit hectic. And surprises. But we did gradually develop a fun social life, split between old high school friends still in the area, new and old faculty friends and of course, family. We would make two or three trips to Overland Park that fall term as well.

One thing that happened soon was the obligatory visit down to the 3rd St. Tavern, hoping to see Wally Galatin, and maybe Jeremiah or other cronies from past days. Word would quickly be about town that we were "slumming it" as DDEC employees, but Wally would tell us not to worry, that a whole lot more scandalous stuff was going on with "certain" folks up at that place. I said, "Cease! We really don't want to know. But you might keep this encounter in mind as just another of the joint 'research' endeavors we both share about Abilene." He laughed, and we had a great conversation over those 25 cent glasses of watery Kansas 3.2 Coors. Some one used to call it "panther piss."

The big news for Wally was Eisenhower's death a year ago now. "I guess for many, and particularly me, it is sad, the end of an era. I helped my father at the studio with early Eisenhower photos, then personally documented in black and white and then color all his visits from 1952 and the opening of his presidential campaign until he became President. There are signed photos as well, and it will all go into that photo book I'm doing."

I guess I could not help but repeat when I "played" Eisenhower on our 4-H Float in that 1952 parade, later got soaked in the rain when he gave his speech out at the old CCC stone stadium, and even stuck my head in the Eisenhower limousine, saying "Hello Ike, Hello Mamie" before they departed. Amazing memories. I guess I needed to bow to national progress and forget personal feelings when his Interstate Highway Bill passed and was implemented, incidentally taking 20 acres off the north end of Dad's farm by 'imminent domain.'"

Wally wanted to know our plans and doings up at the College, and I honestly did not have much to say at that point, just that we were committed to a new start here at home. He said, "I got the idea both you and Mariah were ready to move on back in 1966 after all the excitement here in town. By the way, old – timers still remember your part in nabbing those criminals and you could have run for mayor then. Now, I don't know. Ha ha. Hey, your new 'digs' are not far from me over on 10th street, so we'll have to have some drinks and I'll fill you in on what is *really* happening in Abilene. And speaking of that, is your 'History of Abilene' still in the works?"

"Willy, it has been tabled now for almost three years, but I'm thinking I'll get back to it. What I want to do is delve into the pioneers here and how the town developed. I did the cowboy days and really the Eisenhower days, but I think the key is religion and the twenty – seven churches and the ethnicity of all the farmers. What do you think?"

"You are correct, but there is just as good a story chronicling the businesses in town, and you might stir up a hornet's nest with the whole thing. We did not exactly have 'land battles' like in ranch country out west, but there was plenty of competition and our own 'land – grabbers' just here in the county. I'll give you a tip: go down to the old courthouse and ask to see tax records, go to the 'Reflector' for William Donaldson's stories and then to the library. I think most of the folks involved in the early days are for sure pushing up daisies (oh, you better go out to the cemeteries; I'll go with you), but you should have some second generation old – timers yet around who can talk about it."

Mariah spoke up, "I've heard nary a word about the women in all this and I'll bet my new job that behind every one of those preachers, farmers and bankers was a wife pulling a lot of the puppet strings."

Wally retorted, "I know for sure there were some very colorful and let's say 'exciting' women in Abilene's history, particularly in cowboy days. I'm talking about the respectable Eliza Hersey and the less than respectable but successful Libby Thompson (a famous prostitute and madam of her own house, first here and then on down in Texas), and of course you are right. For the most part, all those upstanding citizens had their wives in appropriate bonnets and Sunday best dresses for church on Sundays. I think the 'in – depth' story on them is yet to be told. Why not a joint book with Mariah handling the female side of things?"

"It would be more interesting if you switched it around; I'll handle the men!" (said feisty Mariah). "On the other hand, I can't think of any man around here, pardon me Mike, who would not enjoy talking to you. Mount up! Keep your powder dry! And watch your topknot! Whoops that's mountain men, not cowboys. Sorry.! Yee haw anyway."

No former high school buddies were in the tavern that night, but Wally said Jeremiah Watson was still around, working in Enterprise, and a smattering of others came home to visit their families from their jobs around central Kansas and the Kansas City area. And there were three or four still farming. So I made a promise to look into all that.

The next week I called the Watson residence, Jeremiah's folks, I think it was a Wednesday, and talked to his mom Stella. We were friends and she remembered both me and Mariah from last time at the church and the long conversation afterwards in their house. "Stella, I still remember those cookies!"

"Mike, there are more from where those came from! Ha. So, Reverend Watson is doing janitorial work up at the college, a new job and better because the hours are regular and the pay steady. We hear you two are back there and at work. I am so happy for you."

"Thanks, Mrs. Watson, we are just getting our feet wet again, busy days, but I'm trying to get hold of Jeremiah. I don't have a phone or address." She said, "Actually he is living here at home now, just the past few months. You know he could not continue down at K – State, just too expensive for the room and board and tuition, and too far and unhandy to drive. He's working in the foundry over at Deershon's in Enterprise, hot and heavy work, but he's all right, and doing some music with a band in Junction City on weekends. I know he will be excited to see you; why don't you call back this evening after 7 and I'll be sure he's here."

"Great, lots of water under the bridge since we were here, but I've got lots to talk to him about. I'll call tonight."

That was Wednesday and we talked that night and decided to meet down at the 3rd Street Tavern on Friday night after he got off work. He said he had a music "gig" over in Junction City Saturday, so Friday would be the best time. It turned out to be a great reunion, he gradually becoming my "best" old friend from town over these last years in Abilene. Mariah had met him, and the two of us had that very moving experience at the church back in 1965 (geez, had it been that long?) Jeremiah looked older, I think his work was taking a bit of a toll on him, or maybe those nights playing the clubs in Junction City. But it was like old times. We had three or four beers (Mariah was "designated" for the drive home just in case) and caught up. He wanted to know all about us, and seeing Mariah's ring, bought another round in congratulations, "About time Mike, about time. Dad, Mom and me all figured it would happen. When, not if."

I asked him about life now the past three years. It was not a real long answer, and in a way a bit sad,

"Mike and Mariah, not much has really changed for me since we were all together. I'm still working at Deershon's over in Enterprise, got a raise or two, so the money for central Kansas is not bad. In a way it keeps me on the straight and narrow; you can't work in a foundry with molten steel and not be on your toes, so it's early to bed and early to rise. My only real entertainment is the band over in Junction. There are four guys, older than I, one terrific girl, Ginni, with a terrific voice (and may I add a terrific physique!). We're doing mainly old Rock n' Roll, some country, but mainly Motown stuff since the crowd is black, soldier boys from Fort Riley, and you still don't want to mix white and black if there's beer and music and women involved. And there are some, what can I say, 'vixens' from Junction who are regulars. We've had to duck flying beer bottles a time or two when things got rough, but we don't have any monopoly on that. The white soldier clubs are the same. The band goes down to Kansas City a couple of times a year to hear 'our peoples' music on 12th and Vine and we even get to sit in now and again, but no worthwhile gigs that we could live on."

"We talked about school back in 1965, any changes on that?"

"Nope. All the same. It's been so long now I don't know if I could get back in the swing of things. I do have almost 24 hours of college credit, mostly those required freshman and sophomore courses, but never was to the point of thinking about a major. I think it takes 30 for the AA two – year degree. I think I told you back then I missed out on any music scholarships. I do think I might be interested some day in maybe teaching music in high school, but you need a degree for that, huh?"

Mariah said, "Where around here do you study for something like that?"

"Oh, K – State or Emporia State have the programs and the requisite music degrees, It would mean at least two more full years' of classes. And that's if you could go full – time. Naah. Can't see it now."

"Jeremiah, let me look into this a bit and see what might be possible, but I'm thinking of something. Have you ever heard of part – time 'adjunct teachers?' Or if not, something less formal. I'll call you in a couple of weeks and will maybe have some news. And one more question: girls. Is there anyone we should know about?"

"Once again, sorry to say there is not. I've got to have something to offer anyone who might be serious, and I don't right now. The only ones in town, and you knew them both in school, Bernice Toomey and her older sister Elisa are off and about to graduate from college. No one interesting, to be honest, is left around Abilene, and I really didn't hang around college long enough to meet anyone. But I'm not broken up about it, there are one or two cute girls from Junction City, both with retired army parents now living in town, and they pop by the club (so far with their chaperones, either Dad or a big brother). That's it."

We had some laughs over old times and I promised to be in touch with any College news. Jeremiah was not too optimistic but said about anything would spice up the work week for him.

3

ON DOWN INTO THE FALL

We were incredibly busy those first few weeks of school, me with classes, Mariah already with a full schedule of office hour appointments from young ladies either needing academic help or trying to make the adjustment to being away from Mom and Dad and out on their own at college. Her reputation evidently preceded her, no doubt nudged by Dr. Halderson and other faculty. How can I say this? I think Mariah really felt needed and was feeling more secure in her/ our decision to come back to DDEC.

Not much to report for me, a bit of a repeat of three years ago: preparation for Spanish classes, coordinating visits from Nara Baldini's high school students to my classes and setting up a fall visit for me to her classes. History, as usual, was far more work, me having to delve into college notes and the books just to have decent lectures in the United States Southwest History course. And I was going to take a big leap and do U.S. History next spring with a four – week component on Kansas and Abilene.

I was able to approach Dr. Halderson about my proposal for Jeremiah Watson teaching music classes at the old Ebenezer First Gospel Church, once each week on a Saturday a.m. for three hours, in exchange for 6 hours credit up at the College in the Spring. Jeremiah's classes would be non – credit of course, but Dr. Halderson added that with no music component at the College, some students with that background and interest would be interested and also, frankly, something fun and wholesome to do outside of the classroom in Abilene. I brought Jeremiah up to meet him, a special appointment on a Saturday morning (Jeremiah all dressed in white shirt, coat, and tie: "Mike, it's just like church with mom and dad"). We talked about Jeremiah's incredible music training at AHS, his talents, his band experience, and some ideas for the informal classes. Dr. Halderson said he could provide the title – "Temporary Adjunct Teacher in Music" – and the class would be listed as an extra – curricular activity in the Spring Schedule. Jeremiah would be enrolled in two night classes for a total of six hours, tuition waived as payment for his informal Saturday morning classes, and the hours would give him the 30 total for the AA degree and a possible move to a music major in the Fall of 1970 at Emporia or K – State.

We worked it all out with his Dad the minister for use of the church on Saturday mornings (the College providing a stipend as "rent" for the morning) and began cooking up lesson plans. Basic music theory, trumpet and – the most fun – impromptu sessions on Country and Gospel music. I agreed to be a regular with my old Kay electric and we could resurrect our old pop – country music "shows" from high school days. Best of all, the Ebenezer Choir would come for the Gospel component. The sessions turned out to not only fulfill our purpose but went beyond anyone's wildest dreams for the community. And, it gave Jeremiah a whole new lease on life (an opinion from his Mom to me and Mariah) and perhaps prospects for the future. He had a model with the Toomey girls; this was **possible!** And there was a reprise for the Saturday night services at church with Reverend Watson preaching, Jeremiah and I doing guitar accompaniment, and students and the church choir singing. Oh, Mariah has a fine voice and she became a mainstay in the group.

And there was more socializing that fall. One big evening was a reunion with what I like to call our "Mexican Connection" in town. For readers of my book on Abilene "Rural Odyssey II – Abilene – Digging Deeper" you will remember Ernie and María González and their kids Mariela and Timmy. After Mariah and I left for school in the East in the Fall of 1966, Timmy even with the AA degree was drafted and is on full – time duty in Viet Nam. He is in a supply corps and at one of the huge bases which offloads materiel to the forces and is safe for now. Mariela who did exceptionally well with us at the Juco is full – time at Emporia State with a scholarship to do a teaching degree for Basic Business and a Spanish Minor. That should set her up for a good job at a high school come graduation this coming Spring.

Since their house is a lot bigger than our apartment, the "welcome back" party was held there. "Tony" Gómez from ice plant days was there as well as his wife and my old friend David García. It was a bit of a reprise of three years ago, lots of chatter (in Spanish), me with my trusty guitar playing the old corny Mexican songs I knew and some "well – oiled" accompaniment by the group, including Mariah with her good voice and ability to sing in harmony (something I never could do). There was plenty of icy cold Mexican beer and, you might have figured, a real feast of María's home cooking (helped by a couple of her local friends) – tacos, enchiladas, tamales (it was close to Christmas time), pico de gallo, arroz, frijol, and flan for dessert. There was a special request by Ernie who led the singing in "Las Mañanitas" and the cheering for our engagement. María gave Mariah a huge hug and then me saying, "Chamaco, sabíamos que ustedes dos iban a casarse, y rezé unas 'Santa Marías' para estar segura. Pues, Nuestra Señora me oyó y cumplió con mi oración. Como la canción, "Dime cuándo, cuándo, cuándo?" Mariah answered for the two of us, "Muy pronto, María, muy pronto."

The evening wore on until the early hours of the next morning, lots of singing and dancing and "vivas" for the upcoming wedding pair. We broke out the guitar again and old Ernie surprised us all with two or three love songs from old Jalisco, saying this is how is courted María. For precaution or whatever, David drove us home with Tony following in his car. No point taking chances these days.

Another event that Fall was when Mariah and I hosted a party (small to be sure) at our apartment for a few International students. Most spoke

Spanish, but not all, so English was the "lingua franca" for the evening. We had ordered out lots of pizza, had plenty of soft drinks on hand and some beer, but keeping a close eye on the kids along that line. Since the legal age in Kansas is 18, and these kids are all college age, no problem there. We talked of how they were getting along, and since the group was small, we already knew their names and something of their families. "Éxito" as Diego Rivera used to say. A success!

On a more personal basis, for old times' sake Mariah and I would go up to the supper club in Salina for a nice meal and dancing, a sentimental place since I guess you could say it was the major spot of our "courting" days. Still no date set for a wedding, but some talk of June of next year. We got out to Mom and Dad's at least every two weeks for a meal, and back out to Ron and Caitlin's just once more that fall. That was when it really dawned on me, at least for the farm, that you "can't go home again." At least regarding that one area.

It was during that second visit we saw all the changes, all for the better for modern farming, but with Dad's farm buildings pretty much disappeared. The chicken house was gone, the hog house as well, and most important the big old barn with the haymow (it had most of the childhood memories I had written about in Rural Odyssey I). But a new hay shed, big feeding troughs for the cattle, sheds for the farm machinery, and a small feed mill and cattle lot up where Dad's windbreak used to be. And of course the new farmhouse.

And incidentally a really nice, crisp if I may say, neatly mowed yard and lane. I think that was the German touch. It looked very nice, enough so I took a lot of pictures, the first the view east down to Highway 40 and the alfalfa field.

Alfalfa Field, the Farm

The Farm Lane

Ron shared all kinds of information with us, mainly filling Mariah in on modern farming. A good visit. We learned that Ron and Stan would eventually change a lot of the planting as well, mainly putting in wheat where the old pasture used to be (no need for that with no horses and cattle now in the feed lot) and cleaning up and sprucing up the pond area. Dad's horse shed and big vegetable garden however were left for him.

Were most other farms modernizing as well around Abilene and Dickinson County? I would have to talk a lot to Ron and Stan, do some drives and maybe talk to more folks in town and at church. More on all that later.

I was still delving into the idea of the Abilene "History" book and there were a half dozen aspects of all that to consider. What I was finding was that both Mariah and I were way too busy with "day to day" tasks, and a project for a book was out of the question. I told her I was so grateful we had finished the dissertations, because I could not imagine teaching, advising and just being a decent human being with that hanging over me. The history book was a little the same way, but I found that conversation was the best avenue to learn.

4

ABILENE - LAW ABIDING
AND RELIGIOUS

At first glance it might not have seemed that way, but often beside the family Bible on the bedside stand or in a drawer underneath was a six – gun or at least a shotgun or rifle in the closet. Since those rowdy, rough cowboy days I described in "Rural Odyssey II," life in Abilene had truly settled down to lots of hard work, but some high-octane religion to go with it. Where to start? I checked the Abilene phone book out of curiosity and there were twenty-seven churches listed for a town of 7000. One Catholic, no Jewish synagogue, no Muslim affiliation, all the rest main - line and other Protestant. I was not able or in fact in any hurry to look into all that, but there are several stories that are important in the history of Abilene.

The town was founded in 1857 and it was no accident the name came from the Bible, Luke, 3. 1. "City of the Plains," a name chosen by pioneers Timothy and Eliza Hersey in 1860. As early as 1857 he ran the store called "Mud Creek" which supplied the Butterfield Overland Stage Line supplies to the west. Their home is preserved in the basement of the Lebold Mansion I wrote about in "Rural Odyssey II." I have not found their specific religious affiliation anywhere, anyway, not yet. But the Biblical connection was surely a sign of things to come.

Not necessarily the most important, but of value because of the preponderance of the Eisenhower name in Abilene is the original family connection. The ancestors on his father's side were Pennsylvania Dutch originally from Germany and settling in York, Pennsylvania in 1741, then Lancaster, and moving to Kansas in the 1880s. His mother Ida was born in Virginia of Protestant ancestry and moved to Kansas in the 1880s as well. Father David and Mother Ida attended Lane College in Lecompton, Kansas, and were married there in 1885. In Abilene both parents were members of the River Brethren sector of the Mennonites. His mother later joined the "International Bible Students Association," later known as Jehovah's Witnesses. From 1896 to 1915 the Eisenhower home was a meeting for the church. Dwight D. never joined but considered himself "deeply religious" and formally was baptized into the Presbyterian Church in 1953. His mother, as appropriate of her religion, was opposed to war, thus reportedly was not happy with Dwight D. going to West Point! What if he had ceded to her wishes? This all is a mouthful!

It's what these different religious affiliations believed that is of interest to Abilene and its evolution. My take from the 1940s to late 1950s: good people are good people no matter what their religious beliefs. I think we must see it all from several angles, but let's start "at home with me." I think I was a bit of a scamp, but also a bit of a "goodie – goodie," partly because of my parents' religion, but mainly due to their own moral make – up. Mom always said, "You cannot and must not ever lie." She said, "Always have a smile for everybody and always say hello to everybody at school." That probably covers most of it, but the Catholic teaching formed all of us kids, like it or not, for better or worse. I detailed all this in many pages in "Rural Odyssey I." You can start with the Apostle's Creed, the basis of our faith (keep in mind I'm writing of all this to put Abilene in perspective):

> I believe in God,
> the Father almighty,
> Creator of heaven and earth,

and in Jesus Christ, his only Son, our Lord,
who was conceived by the Holy Spirit,
born of the Virgin Mary,
suffered under Pontius Pilate,
was crucified, died and was buried;
he descended into hell;
on the third day he rose again from the dead;
he ascended into heaven,
and is seated at the right hand of God the Father almighty;
from there he will come to judge the living and the dead.
I believe in the Holy Spirit,
the holy catholic Church,
the communion of saints,
the forgiveness of sins,
the resurrection of the body,
and life everlasting.
Amen.

It turns out (and much to my surprise) The Creed is used, with variations, in the Catholic, Anglican, Lutheran Moravian, Methodist, and Congregationalist churches. It was the application of all this that created differences. All I know is that Catholics went to mass, believed that Jesus Christ himself was physically present in the blessed bread and wine of the Eucharist, that Confession was a major sacrament, and you were supposed to go to confession, admit your sins, express sorrow and the willingness to pay for them in penance and resolve to not sin again. A big order. Venial sins were okay; mortal sins were life and death. And there was a heaven and hell, and you in your body would end up in one or the other, or maybe "doing time" purging sins in Purgatory with a chance to move up the ladder to heaven.

What caused the big riff, the big difference between Catholics and Protestants, rarely spoken among us school kids, or even known, was Rome.

Rome. Rome. Rome. And all the rules, regulations and traditions that came out of it. Our entire national history since the Pilgrims' desire for religious freedom (not just from Rome, but European Crowns who told you what to believe and do) formed this dichotomy then and now. In many cases, if you disagreed or did not believe, you started your own church. Where do I start, or end for that matter? For the Catholics, Sunday mass or daily mass, confession of sins to a priest, Holy Communion, not eating meat on Fridays, fasting on Ash Wednesday and Good Friday and abstaining from meat during Lent, Holy Days of Obligation, priests not marrying, the hierarchy of Catholic clergy from the local priest to the bishop to the cardinals to the Pope at the top. The Pope, hmm. Infallible? There was a joke in my school days in Abilene by the Protestant kids, "Is the Pope a Catholic? Does a beat shit in the woods?" Few knew what that big word "infallible" meant, including many Catholics. But there was the practical side; Catholics were from Southern Europe originally and then from Ireland, Germany and France. Alcohol was not forbidden and was a part of daily life for many. And, yes, dancing. Even close dancing, cheek to cheek.

We Catholic kids didn't know what all our Protestant buddies and girlfriends believed because you never talked about it. A good thing and just as well. But the Catholics knew that a lot of the Protestant kids were not supposed to drink alcohol, smoking was not a good thing for anyone but was common (no national cancer warnings yet at that time), and some groups like some of the Southern Baptists were discouraged from dancing, and all of us were expected to marry our own. Oh yeah, a "mixed" marriage, and I am talking religion, was extremely rare. And we are not even talking of race or skin color; that was beyond the horizon.

I think all the religions, Catholic and whatever Bible Belt Protestant version you might imagine, discouraged pre – marital sex, and masturbation was material for young guys' jokes or "verboten." Being "moral" was one thing; but another was having a car, necking in the back seat at the drive in, or more likely the front if there were no gear shift from the floor from the middle. Am I stirring up any memories for possible readers? There was no sex education in the schools. Ha! Who handled it? Parents? Churches? Farm animal examples? Or peer talk and jokes? The guys had stories of always keeping a "rubber" or condom in your billfold, for just in case. I never did. One thing now as I write this is the big news: THE PILL! Unwanted pregnancies happened up through the 1950s and 1960s, and religion was not the main matter; it was pure hormones. Girls "went away" and returned home, but unhappily everyone "knew." The Catholic orphanages were famous for taking in the "orphans." We did not know what the Protestant people did. I know they had the equivalent of those old nuns' orphanages. There were adoption agencies. But I do not know if I ever heard the word "abortion" growing up. I never heard Mom, Dad, Caitlin or Ron ever mention any of this.

I need to get Mariah's take on all this.

Have I covered it all? I doubt it, but *these* were the issues and the social, religious mores that governed life in Abilene in those "innocent years." All I know is that kids grew up, the hormones grew stronger, boys began to feel those fluids, girls bloomed, and it was a lot of fun. And now, in 1969, the times are changing. Once again, I considered doing an in-depth history of all those twenty-seven churches, but yes or no, the bottom line would be the paragraphs I just wrote. I was not about to go around doing surveys of beliefs and stirring up emotions or troubles, and to top that off, I did not have the time anyway. I am sure among adults of diverse religious persuasions there was unspoken disagreement, even animosity, maybe some jealousy or envy, but also amazing tolerance with the goal of just "getting along" and leaving each to his own.

Related, but not related, basically all you had to do was talk to anyone in Abilene about their last name or where they went to church, and you had the story of both ethnicity and religion in Abilene. Or better yet, go to the phone book. We had them all it seemed – German, Dutch, Irish, Scotch, English, Swedish, Danish, Russian, a smattering of French and Italian. And of course a small Mexican contingent and Negro as well. And I don't know who I'm leaving out. The final arbiters were the tombstones in the cemeteries, Catholic and Protestant. As I told Mariah in our many discussions, you did not even discuss or talk much about religion outside your family as a kid. You had your Catholic friends because you grew up with them at church. And they were the numerical minority. There were no Catholic or Protestant schools, just public (a very good thing I believe). The Protestant kids? You did not go to church with them, and you weren't in DeMolay or Job' Daughters, so the subject just did not come up. Maybe that's why we all got along so well.

5

ECONOMICS AND SOCIAL CLASS IN TOWN

Economics, meaning being poor or wealthy or somewhere in between, is yet another matter for any "History of Abilene." There were ramifications for Mariah and me that Fall. It was economics however that was the basis for the social structure in town yet in 1969. And there is nothing wrong with that; it is a fact of life. Where to start? Where you lived, where you went to school, where you worked, in some cases where you shopped, and certainly your social connections all revolved around economics or, in part, your religion. The "wealthy, middle or poor" parts of Abilene had not really changed since the 1940s and 1950s, except that now there was the beginning of a move out of town to nearby rural areas for I think the upcoming generation of children of Abilene's "old" upper echelon folks. Think about it: kids don't want to live with their parents and if they have the resources will move out on their own. Not related to this, but an important other major factor was that many of the area's children had gone away to school or to the military and gotten on with their new lives outside of town and never returned. Incidentally, it was this latter phenomenon that Dr. Halderson and others were trying to fight: give these kids an education and the skills and opportunities to create new jobs around Abilene and in the county.

So there were new housing neighborhoods from converted farm land, east of Brady Street on the east side of town, north of town on Highway 15 beyond the old orphanage and St. Joseph's Dairy, south out by the Smokey Hill and east toward Enterprise. And several farms and farmhouses were purchased from folks ready to retire, the houses remodeled or torn down and built anew. Just one case in point I guess was Dad and Mom's farm and farmhouse. I did know some of the people involved in the new trend in building (Mariah not so much, but some from our first stay as teachers at the old Juco). A good part of them were kids I grew up with, the children who inherited old mom and pop businesses in Abilene or others who were new to town: professionals - medical doctors, new lawyers in town - and maybe a few teachers from the new DDEC. More than once Mariah and I were asked if we were going to buy a nice house or join the local move to build one. Our answer was like the wedding date, "Not yet. No hurry." We did not elaborate that we were just out of school and did not have much in the way of savings. We at least wanted to rent through most of that first year back at the college. Also, what we did not say to anyone and really did not yet address ourselves quite yet was if this year was a test to see if we would stay.

A second question was if we would be wanting to join the local country club, if we played golf or tennis (and they had a private swimming pool, as opposed to the big public pool out in Eisenhower Park, the one we used when I lived on the farm). I think DDEC people were considered for membership, and I discovered it was not all just a gratuitous thought – the Country Club was hurting as well for membership, not cheap to keep that beautiful golf course green and dining and social area in a big two story ranch house. We also demurred on that, diplomatically saying we were just getting our feet on the ground again, and not saying that neither of us were "country club folks."

We did however join the Elks Club mainly because of the monthly dinner – dances and due to the fact that Dad was a long – time member, Ron's family as well, and a lot of the Catholic businessmen in town including Mr. Storz at the Abilene National Bank, the Zolls from the grocery stores, the German - Catholic who owned one of the drug stores, and some farm families. The Elks Hall was an important place for wedding receptions, 50th anniversary celebrations and the like. I truly did not nor do not know now if many of its members were in the Abilene Country Club, but I do know that many of the town's doctors and lawyers were Elks members; Dad played Gin Rummy with some of them on Sundays.

A lot of the above reflects thinking from growing up; unfortunately, Mariah's family, for altogether different reasons (Jewish ethnicity) were not asked by such places for membership, a touchy subject in certain circles (it was called blackballing and Mariah had experienced it during rush week at sororities at K.U.) that is, except the very large eastern cities where Jewish folks had their own clubs. This was not apropos for us anyway since most townspeople, at least for a long time, did not know she was Jewish. We both basically had other social priorities, to be seen soon enough, but Spanish language and culture, and counseling of many underprivileged students would be among them.

As well as the new housing construction, a lot of fixing up, remodeling or at least painting went on in the old established part of town, a big case in point the sprucing up of the old Seelye Mansion and large Victorians on Buckeye and West 3rd street. A small but upscale new neighborhood had developed just east of the High School. The other side of the coin was that there were a few boarded up store fronts downtown. Locals would tell us, gradually, that it was the farm situation that indirectly caused this. The stores I remembered like the drug stores, the small food markets, the big RHV complex, Duckwall's Five and Dime, the movie theaters, barber shops and beauty salons, banks, insurance companies and the old United Trust, were mostly still in business. The old famous Sunflower Hotel had long ago been converted into apartments, but there were two or three modest motels on the west side and a spanking brand new one on north Buckeye near the Interstate. Tourism and the Eisenhower Complex were no small movers in that. There was a new, small "business park" out west of the fairgrounds, the big "hitter," Russell Stover Candy Company. Everyone joked about working there, wondering about the "candy" breaks along with "coffee breaks."

And the other neighborhoods; they were, in effect, not necessarily poor except in a few cases, but rather, modest. Southeast Abilene both above and below the Union Pacific Tracks and rail yard, small residential areas south and southwest of downtown, and a smattering north of the old athletic field and football stadium and in spots west of Mud Creek but beyond the old, big homes on west 3rd; these were all cases in point. But it is dangerous to generalize; nice tree shaded middle class homes could be all over and in any part of town. All Abilene took great pride in our town, and most all regardless of job or income tried to keep things in order.

What is left? I'll do a whole other part on farms near town or in the county.

6

EVENTS ABOUT TOWN

That Fall was marked once again by routine the reader of "Rural Odyssey II" already is familiar with: the Turkey Shoot out at the Wassman's farm on the river bottom outside of town, "obligatory" football games of old AHS, occasional school plays, and church socials. And I think I mentioned that for old times' sake we would drive over to Salina to the dance – supper club back in early "courting" days. Sometimes friends from the College would go with us, Jenny from the English Department and her husband, Joel Adams from History and his wife Emily. We would regularly socialize with them. Ron and Caitlin even went along one time, laughing that they had done the same courting at the same place ten years before. And with the same idea: keep Abilene busybodies and gossips from prying into their affairs.

The citizens in Abilene were not having the problems I wrote about in "Rural Odyssey II" from three years ago, the vandalism, church damage, cemetery damage and the culmination down at the Eisenhower Museum, that was a good thing. But there were still occasions when William Donaldson down at the paper could do headlines. Mainly accidents.

A careless participant, maybe with a drink too many, wounded himself in the leg out at the Turkey Shoot in October. He was getting ready to shoot skeet, must have been unsteady enough that he slipped, and the gun went off, a pretty bad flesh wound to his lower leg. An ambulance was out from town in just a bit, they wrapped the leg and had him settled down in the hospital that evening. Fortunately, it was late afternoon when it happened, and most of the shooting and socializing had finished by then. Before that it was the usual homemade pies and cake and hot coffee (very cool fall weather with everyone in jackets or even light coats, me for sure with a stocking cap). Mariah and I were greeted by everyone, and I told her later that that was the first time I really felt like I was "back home," that is, other than Mom and Dad, Caitlin and Ron, and friends up at the College. The event was a great memory going back to early teenage years. Most everyone knew Mariah, and all the ladies came up, admired her ring and wanted to know the latest. Since this was a basically a church affair, although sportsmen came from all over the county, both the men and women knew us. I think Mom was proud as a peacock and maybe a bit frustrated she did not have more news to share with her church lady friends. That leads me to think of the great talk Mariah and I had with Father Kramden down at St. Andrew's later that fall and also our reunion with Sheriff Wiley.

Before I get into either of those though, more "current events." One involved teenagers; evidently some high school kids got "oiled up" on 3.2 Coors during one of the home football games and were drag racing down Buckeye when there was a near head - on collision. One of the kids swerved over into the left oncoming lane and bashed in the left fender and side of a car. Not a good thing. Sheriff Wiley and Police Chief Sampson were there right away, sirens blaring, an ambulance from the hospital just a few blocks away. The oncoming car's sole driver was whisked off to the hospital and fortunately without serious injury. The kids were taken down to the police station and cited for reckless driving, but apparently not for DWI, a bit strange under the circumstances. It reminded me of an incident at college in Kansas City, Missouri during undergraduate days – it was one of the big city kids from St. Louis when we were all over on the Kansas side at Sammy's Bar. He was drunk as a hoot owl and was loudly boasting, "You can't get drunk on this 3.2 shit," He was very drunk indeed. Case closed.

The "Reflector Chronicle" also had what I surmise is an annual story of the vandalism that takes place the night of Halloween, generally an innocent state of affairs. Someone paints the water tower and there are still outhouses on some properties around town and they get turned over. Rarely is anyone physically hurt, but old William Donaldson feels like the citizens expect a report.

Far more serious later in the Fall was the event out on the Interstate when a big 18-wheeler flipped over in the median; the driver was thrown out and suffered a broken neck. There was no official "cause" of the wreck in the article in the paper the next day except for a highway patrolman's off the cuff remark that the long haul driver may have fallen asleep at the wheel. We always understood in those days that the drivers would drive over their allotted hours, taking those little white "speed" tablets to get them home after several days on the road. But that was all conjecture and "talk;" I nor anyone I was around knew any drivers.

Sheriff Wiley was at that skeet shoot, as always, and the reader knows we go way back from the Eisenhower Center incident. I had taken Mariah to visit him a time or two before when we were visiting the folks when we were home from back east college days. He urged us to come on down, I said it would have to be a Saturday, so we set it up for the a.m. of the following Saturday.

Events up at the College intervened that week, Mariah's first crisis as Dean of Women. We got the call about 10:00 p.m. on a Tuesday. Apparently one of the young coeds, a freshman from the tiny town of Beloit in north central Kansas, evidently tried to commit suicide. Her roommate found her comatose, the roommate just returning to the room from the college library. They rushed the girl, one Jamie Swenson, to the hospital and pumped out her stomach, full of sleeping pills she evidently ingested earlier that evening. Wendy her roommate was in near hysterics, but when we got to the hospital (and Wendy was there with Jamie), she just sobbed on Mariah's shoulder saying it was all her fault. She knew Jamie had been depressed for days, not doing well in classes, unable to concentrate, but only said it was "trouble at home." They gave Wendy a sedative and asked her to return home to the dorm, but Mariah stayed for three hours at the hospital with Jamie, and only piled into bed well after midnight. I would get the story only the next day. Basically, it was just a dismal situation – the parents getting a divorce, no brothers or sisters for moral support, and money a real problem. Mariah somehow talked her through the immediate crisis, put her on a regular "watch list" up at school, and we had her over to the house (our apartment) several times over the next few weeks for "girl talk" and what amounted to counseling. Jamie was able to finish the term, and Mariah looked into school financial support that enabled her to continue in the Spring. As the year went along, there were other emergencies, but all mainly handled up at school either in the infirmary, or one on one meetings Mariah would arrange between a teacher and troubled student.

I asked her if this was what she had in mind getting the degree and taking this job with its duties (I think I used the word "headaches," that was a mistake!). Mariah said, "Look, I'm new at this and am perhaps learning as I go, but Mike I really believe I'm making a difference and that I have something, a knack, a gift, for this sort of thing. Don't, please, ever use that word again, okay?"

"Okay, for sure. I think I always knew you were wired for such things. And I'm proud of you."

The rest of the week rolled on by, pretty much routine for the both of us, and I reminded Mariah that I especially wanted to check in with Sheriff Wiley again, so we were in in office with the usual bad coffee at 9:00 Saturday morning. He got up from his desk, shook hands with me and gave Mariah a big smile, "Hey I heard you folks finally decided to get hitched. Congratulations. About time. When's the date?"

"Not set yet, Wiley, but we will let you know. We just wondered how it is going, what's new and if there's anything we ought to know?"

"Geeze, Mike, when did we talk? I think it was about a year ago on one of your visits home. It has really been pretty much routine around here, no murders, no kidnappings, one suicide of a farmer out west of Solomon and the sad funeral, and just the occasional family quarrel at home we get called for, but those turn out to be dicey. A couple may hate each other and be at each other's throat, one calls us, but when we get there, *we* are the bad guys. There have been some close calls over the years. Oh, I got reelected again last year, so four more years before I have to go through the hand shaking and baby kissing routine, but you know in all honesty I've done a decent job. And the Eisenhower Museum affair in that odd sense didn't do any harm. You want to be a part – time deputy? I can do it tomorrow."

I laughed and said I and Mariah had enough on our plates, but asked what else was on his mind, or his watch list.

"Mike and Mariah, we've had none of that nasty separatist or KKK stuff since 1966, and no notification by the FBI or KBI of any suspicious activity in the county. The jerks, may I say, Neanderthals, seem to have quieted down or gone into their caves since the bombing here and troubles up in Idaho in '66. We are however concerned about anti – war stuff by the radicals from Chicago last summer, violent demonstrations or the like, and the mess in Viet Nam is not getting any better, but no local problems. In regard to the War and the separatists, they claim to be great patriots. On the other hand, they don't want to be beholden to any government, local or national, or have the feds telling them what to do, so I imagine that includes a government war. I reckon there are quite a few draft dodgers up there across the border in Canada. But back to the local stuff, there is the occasional vandalism, break – in, car theft or gas station robbery, but with Salina and Junction City help, and KBI we keep it to a minimum. But, hey, it's sure good to see the two of you, have you back in town, and I hear nothing but good things about your work up at the College. And Mariah, you get a gold star for helping out the coed the other day; in case you don't know, we are apprised of all hospital ins and outs."

Mariah thanked Wiley, we concluded that "no news was good news," and I said we'd be seeing him down at church now and again, and that we had been wanting to talk to Father Kramden just to catch up. Wiley said he saw his car over there just this morning, so I talked Mariah into going on over for that "catch up" visit.

7

CONVERSATION AT ST. ANDREW'S

We learned that theologian Robert Hater is the expert on interfaith marriages, and Father Kramden gave us some ideas to discuss and recommended reading Hater's book, a "wealth of knowledge on the subject." It would at least set us straight on the practices, if not the rules, and would give us a lot to chew on. Father Kramden gave us his take on it all.

"When one partner is not Catholic or Christian, as in Mariah's case, there is something called 'Disparity of Marriage,' and a Bishop has to approve the ceremony. The Catholic partner has 'to make a sincere promise to do all in his or her power for the children to be baptized and raised Catholic.' If the non – Catholic insists that the children not be raised Catholic or that they be given their own choice, the marriage can still happen with the Diocesan approval, but the Catholic is still bound by the promise 'To do all he/or she can … .' Then it all starts to get complicated. For instance, if Mariah wanted a Rabbi to be present at the ceremony, that is fine, but the Catholic priest must officiate. Bottom line, such marriages happen all the time and things can be worked out, but 'Holy Mother Church' cautions that all may become very difficult.

"So, what happens when either person is not a practicing person in their respective faiths? One option would be a wedding, a ceremony but no mass. I think that is your best bet."

Mariah was quick to speak up, "This has really been a help, Father. Mike and I will talk, and honestly, I've got to talk to my parents. There is going to have to be some give and take and a lot of discussion, but I think we can figure it out."

That was in the end a very likely scenario. It would happen.

8

THE FARMING COMMUNITY

If I were going to persist in a "History of Abilene," or maybe now, in some less complicated version of the same in maybe just a long article form, it would be necessary to tackle the reality all of us in Abilene were facing: the old and new changing times on the farms. Once again, I discovered that I had neither the time nor really the motivation to get permission to go through tax records and slug through land sales at the courthouse but soon discovered that long talks with my own relatives and friends, Dad's farm friends and others they introduced me to would provide the basis for what I say in this book. I was not so sure about the actual Abilene History Book; too much on my plate up at the college.

One of the friends was Clay Wommer and his wife Carolyn who invited us over for barbecued hamburgers out in the back yard, and we were reintroduced and reminisced over past and present times. Both Clay and Carolyn were in my high school class and Clay and I shared long – time sports teams from the days he used to play basketball for Talmage Grade School and me for Garfield, and then on into junior high and maybe freshman years at AHS. Funny, I remember him wearing his FFA (Future Farmers of America) jacket to high school; I never did join up, lucky as I was to just help out Dad with chores all year long and farm work in the summer without hurting myself. It was a long evening and there was a lot to cover, the details on farm talk on yet another a.m. when Clay and I sat over coffee in the kitchen of their totally remodeled house in town. Clay, ahem, was handy! As was Carolyn. I don't recall for sure if it was Clay or his dad who had sold the farm, much like my dad, so we would compare notes and "takes" on that. They had young children, so life was a handful with work and the kids. They were both a treasure trove of information on the general economic and social changes not only in Abilene, but in the county. Carolyn ran for and was elected to be one of the county officials, so that explained the county news.

They knew about Mariah from our previous time at the old Juco but were excited to hear our news of the engagement and our plans. Our mantra, "Not yet. Not yet. But soon." They caught us up on any old friends, high school classmates still living in Abilene, and Carolyn knew all about the girls from high school, whom they had married, where they were living, how many kids they had. There was a bit of joking and laughter about those innocent days I wrote about in "Rural Odyssey." They were very curious as to how things were up at the "college" as everyone in Abilene called it. We could recount our experience from before when it was just the "juco," but it was too early to have much to add now in the Fall of 1969.

Incidentally, things were not so quiet on the national and international fronts either. It all seemed so distant from Abilene, but there were race riots in Hartford, Connecticut, and the Trial of the Chicago 7 in late September. We all were against national violence and upheaval, and the general view in Abilene was that the "mess" in Chicago was all caused by anti – war people, both black and white. No one was too ready to talk about the latter, just saying they thought we were way in over our heads over there in Asia. The main thing I remember is that the national TV news with Walter Cronkite at 5:30 had the "body count" of deaths and prisoners, including Vietnamese captured. I'll leave it at that.

We did talk about the "Pill" with Mariah and Carolyn taking the lead on that, both expressing it was new but for sure welcome. The Wommers wanted my take on it, knowing I was Catholic, but being basically uninformed I just said I thought the starvation and excess of world population especially in the Third World might have been a lot different if the pill had come along fifty years ago! Machismo notwithstanding. And I surmised there were many families in the U.S. ready for the family planning it could bring. And I thought it was women who should take the lead on it. This first conversation was in late September 1969.

Another source, one I got from a suggestion from my Dad, was Mr. Dyson, one of the old farmers northeast of town not far from Grandma O'Brien's original acres and a good friend of Dad's who helped to fill in the blanks. We had a long conversation over coffee on a Saturday morning. He knew my Dad well enough to know each of their lives. Both had sold their farms in the early1960s after I had graduated from high school, and it turns out for similar reasons. He said, "I was getting near retirement age, tired both in my bones and mentally dealing with the farm hassles. You can put it all in a nutshell: farm commodities were at a low, maybe not as much as the mid-1950s during the drought years (which I remembered and talked about in "Rural Odyssey"), that included both grain and livestock prices." His farm was very similar to Dad's: they both were almost self- sufficient in growing food in big vegetable gardens, butchering livestock for meat including beef and pork, and having chickens for eggs and eating as well. And milk cows provided milk and cream.

"The big 'kicker' was the farm machinery; it was getting old and wearing out, almost impossible to keep repaired. A new, decent tractor capable of all the field work was a sky-high price and a harvester (for wheat and corn) even more, this in 1962. Upland acreage was up in price a little, maybe $400 per acre, and it just seemed a good idea to sell for a good price and retire to a small house in town." But Mr. Dyson had farm skills and knew farming, so was lucky to find a regular job down at the big grain elevator south of the Union Pacific Tracks, doing maintenance, long hours at the mill during harvest, and then regular work at the docks for whenever the farmers came into town and needed to sell or buy.

I asked him, "Do you miss the farm?"

He thought a bit, then smiled and laughed. "I miss the outdoors, the smell of the soil turned over during plowing, the smell of fresh cut alfalfa, and funny enough, the smell of the barnyard. I miss getting the single – shot or shotgun to go rabbit hunting. I miss the whole thing of getting the soil ready for planting wheat in the fall, hoping for fall rains to get it started, hoping it makes it through the winter, the spring wind and rain or not, and then it greening up, heading out and getting ready for harvesting. Same with alfalfa and corn. I do not miss getting up every day at 5:00 in the morning, doing chores and then going to the field, same in the afternoon, and too darned tired to enjoy much before bedtime. And I miss being my own boss. But, Mike, there was no way we were going to make a good living and ever be free of debt. I could tell you of at least ten friends from then and now who could tell the same story. I'm thinking of Grady Zimmerman as well, moved into town, working at the Co - op, his wife is at the Peoples' bank. Or maybe Clay Wommer as well."

"And we had a death a while back out east of town between here and Detroit. The paper called it a hunting accident, but Roy Goodwin was found dead one morning from a shotgun wound to the head. Fortunately, Roy was not married and left no children, but it was sad, so sad. We all knew him, a good young man who had inherited his Dad's half section a couple of miles east of the County Farm east of your Dad's old place. But I know personally his equipment was old and spent, he had no cattle operation, and with low crop prices, high expenses and little rain last year I'm thinking it just all became too much. There was a huge crowd down at St. Andrew's, your Dad was one of the pall bearers, and I think more farmers were there that day than any time lately in Abilene, and that includes the county fair and rodeo. Roy was a tackle on the AHS football team, served three years in the Army, but just never had married, I'm guessing because he did not believe he had much to offer a prospective wife. But Mike, that's just one story. Most farmers have been able to hang on, and some have prospered, adapting to be sure to the current markets."

I spoke of brother – in – law Ron's story, his buying the house and farm from Dad, and seeing all the changes he had made and a bit of the emotional toll that had taken on me. Mr. Dyson said, "Pardon me, but there is a whale of difference there from me and your Dad's situation, and I'm not telling you anything you do not already know. Ron and Stan both have college degrees in milling technology and had the means to get funding for their feed lot. Stan is farming some of best land in Dickinson County, that river bottom land south of town. And even your Dad's land was kind of a mix with some good flat land a way up from the river and upland; we were all upland."

"Yeah, Mr. Dyson, I know, and another big factor was simple – irrigation. We could neither afford it nor really had the right acreage to do it. The old Schmidt farm south of town was perfect, and Stan and Ron inherited all the irrigation equipment plus the water wells to do it."

"You bet. It's another world south of town, or anywhere along the river, west and east of town. Believe me, I know from experience just keeping my eyes open around town at the feed stores and at the flour mill because you see all the farmers, rich and poor, some driving big, shiny new pickups and with big new grain trucks, others 1950s vintage Fords or Chevy's, and small grain trailers."

"Mr. Dyson, you might remember from just a few years ago, that business of the buyers of land up in the north county who turned out to be connected to a big syndicate of KKK money. I guess you knew a few of the local farmers. My question, is it the big corporations who are buying most of the small old farms today?"

"No, not really, at least around Abilene. And pardon me again, it's the successful farm operations like Ron and Stan's and the Windstroms out west of town, and the old families out in the river bottoms with big bank accounts and kids who can run the operations. With the new equipment, there is a whole new setup for transporting equipment, tractors, plows, cultivators, and threshers, so these new folks can farm profitably all around the country, river bottom, upland and in between. You know, Mike, I read your 'Rural Odyssey;' got a copy down at the Dickinson County Historical Society. That was a way of life which has gone by the boards, we remember it and cherish it, but there's no going back. You made some mistakes in that book, but on the whole, it did tell the story."

"Mr. Dyson, I am sorry and apologize for the mistakes, but like I said in the book, I wrote it while not living here anymore, and with the memory in charge, and a lot of water had gone under that bridge. Can't really help it now."

9

THE REAL SCOOP AND I DO NOT MEAN MANURE

My main source and maybe the most informative for modern farming around Abilene and all the changes was brother – in – law Ron Schmidt. Most of what I'm writing took place in a long conversation out at the farmhouse east of town on a Sunday afternoon, and Mariah was there to hear it all. We had enjoyed a big Sunday afternoon meal and Mom and Dad were there, and we were all gathered in the living room. The kids were either taking naps or playing outside, and Mom and Dad have gone back into town, time for his nap too. Maybe just as well since some of the talk may or may not have been a bit painful to him. Why? We were talking a lot about Ron and Stan's changes to the old place and changes in the "new world of farming" as Ron put it.

I started off, trying to choose my words as best I could, saying it was hard for me to see the old place with the house and barn gone, the windbreak north of the house, but on the other hand how good the place now looked. Grass neatly clipped along highway 40 with new mailboxes, the same on the neatly mown and well graveled lane up to the house, the manicured large lawn and trees and the pretty red – bricked house. Ron smiled, saying he was wondering how I would take all that, but that he was happy with what I'd said. He then explained his view on the changes:

"Mike, Stan and I have basically done a thirty year change from when your Dad started here in the early 1940s, and in many ways the same thing out by the river with my dad's old farm and that of all the Schmidt brothers and old neighbor families like the Baxtroms and the Rebensdorfs. If you give me a few minutes, I'll explain, okay? (I said yes.) First of all, the house. Even though it was over 100 years old, it basically was falling down structurally, that old limestone foundation was crumbling (I agreed, saying I could remember the powder if you ran your fingers through the mortar between the stones), the asbestos siding looked okay but was dangerous for your health. There are studies now the damned stuff can cause cancer if anyone is exposed to it long enough! And farmers all over the county had put that stuff on their old clapboard houses to dress them up. And the old wooden 2 X 4s, roof beams and floor joists were rotting. Mike, that was basically a no – brainer if we were to live on the farm. I'm glad you like the looks of the new place.

"The old barn, as historic as they are all over Kansas, had the same problems, old 2 x 4s, roof beams and joists in the loft floor, the old side boards weathered and rotting, and the roof an accident waiting to happen. (I said I remembered seeing all the holes in it when we used to stack hay up there or I was tossing bales down to the livestock or even playing basketball on the wooden floor and backboard.) Same thing with the old chicken house and hog house."

I said, "Just the same, I'm glad I wrote all about it in my book 'Rural Odyssey.' The memories are all there. But why did you get rid of the windbreak? Dad planted and nurtured every one of those trees. And I know they served their purpose with the Kansas windstorms and blizzards."

"Mike, once again, we'll go outside north of the granary and you will see that not all of them are gone, and there are still enough to serve that purpose. But with our change to traditional farming (which you knew) plus a good-sized cattle feeding operation, I needed space. You have seen the original corral and the concrete feeders we put in, but we had to put the mill next to that to the north, and that's where I felled about one – half the trees. Many were dying, others matted with weeds; we saved the best. Mike, I know you are not a technical guy, but both Stan and I have college degrees in Milling Technology from maybe the best program in the country down at K – State. When we made the decision to put that to use, it was a whole new ball game. Let me just give you the 'short list' of what we needed: feeding system, feed delivery, feed storage, silage pits, hay storage, feed processing mill, feed mixing/batching, feed trucks, feed alleys and feed bunks."

"Damn! I'm glad that's the short list!"

"I won't bore you with the details, but maybe you and Mariah can do the quick tour north of the granary sometime and it will make a lot more sense. And this was for what we call today just a small to medium feeding operation of about 400 head of cattle. And you have to keep your herd healthy, doctored, and renewed each year. You heard the 'ole Kenny Rogers' song, 'The Gambler' - 'Know when to hold 'em, know when to fold 'em.' It's the same with cattle, kind of a poker game, but instead of the other guys' hands, it is the weather, the vagaries of grain and feed production, government regulations, and the market. Know when to buy 'em and know when to sell 'em. We've been right most of the time, but not all the time. But maybe now you know why I get up every day at 4:30 to get a jump on things."

Mariah had sat patiently, the city girl, but with a head for business and administration I didn't have, nodding her head in affirmation. Ron noticed this, smiled, and said, "Mike, you got a good one there. Two heads are better than one." We all laughed, and Ron suggested we all get a beer or a glass of wine and he would give us "Part II."

"What I have told you is just the half of it. The rest is why I need Stan, his resources, and the fact we can work together and pool knowledge, funds and hard work to make this all a go. I hate to use another analogy, but this one is from the stock market: you've got to hedge. By that I mean, just simply, is to balance your traditional farming operation of raising wheat, alfalfa and corn and storing and selling your crops for the best price you can get and keeping some part of it for feed for your cattle. Hell, we are not magicians, but you can figure it takes some doing and good timing. And maybe some luck. That's why we kept your Dad's original silo, built two new enclosed ones to store forage for milling, and added steel grain bins to hold excess corn and wheat to see if we could beat the market. And, oh yeah, that big, long hayshed where the chicken house used to be. Another cliché: buy low and sell high, ha, most of the time."

"My head is spinning, but I think I get it, and it all is making a lot more sense to me now. There's one more thing on my mind and I'm sure you are getting at it soon enough – the machinery and farm equipment to get it all done."

The John Deere Dually

We'll go out for a look at the machinery later; it's all in the storage sheds north of the granary and southeast of the mill. We don't store anything out in the open weather, and besides, it makes for a neat, clean operation. We mainly need a tractor with a front-end loader for putting feed in the feed troughs and handling manure and such, another big tractor to do all the field work plus a plough, a big disk and a cultivator, a good mower and rake for the hay, a baler, and they now have big harvesters that can do both wheat and corn. And a couple of trucks, one for miscellaneous stuff at the feed lot, another for grain. You make do with mostly old machinery, replacing it when you can't fix it, and gradually replacing with new. We've found used machinery doesn't cut it, always breaks down too soon and just isn't reliable. You can see our new big John Deere Dually tractor with a cab and the new grain harvester. They cost more than two new houses in Abilene."

Mariah said, "And how much is that?" (You could see the brain working.)

Ron laughed, "Enough that you better be on good terms with the bankers in town. We have an advantage over a lot of folks because Dad and my uncles, and Mike's Dad for that matter, had good solid reputations in town for paying their bills. If you were a young farmer starting up, you would either have to have a big bankroll or someone else to co-sign for you. It's curious which banks you use, but it is almost always based on what your Dad used, or maybe church or social connections. For us that's the Catholics or the Elks. Farming is a different enterprise; you can extrapolate future prices and estimate yields, but that's a crap shoot. You know costs will go up (Have you ever seen a price go down?) and not necessarily livestock or grain prices. So that's why past record and "good will" probably rule the day. Mr. Storz down at the Abilene National Bank is a long-standing member of St. Andrew's and we've got friends at the 'Peoples' Bank. So there you go."

Mariah said, "Hmm. A lot different than buying a house in town. I guess the bankers look mainly then at your tax returns and salaries; is that right? And of course, your credit rating. Makes it hard when you are starting out."

"Yeah, that's why it's a good idea for you guys to buy a car or pickup truck or even appliances on time (as if most people have a choice), just to get the ball rolling. In you guys' case, I would guess good standing in the community with two jobs up at the college would be a good starting point. But you can see a house and a farm are apples and oranges, or as they used to say, 'a horse of a different color.' By the way, what's going on with all that?"

Mariah took the lead. "Ron, we're just back for our first year with jobs with some new duties, and we really have to see how it goes. We're getting on through half of the year but will have to see what spring term brings. And we don't even have a date yet for the wedding although June sounds nice. We do have a Jewish custom I'd like to follow, an out of doors wedding. And on a Sunday afternoon. But that's all up in the air; we haven't got the Catholic – Jewish customs mix straightened out yet."

"Well, Caitlin and I can offer you the first gift – our big front and back lawns, plenty of room for tables and chairs and tents for the weather. And a beautiful farm scene looking out east and down to the highway. Just a thought. Oh, and if the wind is blowing in the right direction, no barnyard smell. Ha."

I guess it was my turn. "Thanks, Ron. How did we get from cattle and feedlots to weddings? Whoa. One thing at a time. Don't want to get the cart before the horse on this deal, although maybe Mariah wants, what is it in 'Oklahoma?' a surrey with the fringe on top! Yee haw. Just kidding. So back to the machinery, what are we talking about for a new tractor or combine?"

"Are you ready? The dually cost over $100,000 in 1963 when we bought your Dad's farm (a lot more than the farm in fact); the new harvester last year was $150,000. And mostly gradual other stuff since 1963. Lots of changes, Mike. We now use chisel plows, and those old sickle hay mowers, rakes, and block and tie or automatic balers are long gone. The current thinking in plowing is to not expose the turned over soil from old – style plowing to our winds, so just break up the stubble enough with the chisel to allow rain to penetrate the soil and plant. You might have to disk to break up the stubble, but it cuts out the harrowing. But the biggest change is the haying equipment. We hardly lift a bale; it's all stacked from the new baler and we have a pick-up to load it onto wagons or trucks. It's all new words too: the old mower is now a windrower; the bales go on the ground and are picked up with an accumulator and either stacked on trucks for direct sale or on truck or trailer beds to be off lifted and stacked in the barns."

"Ron, my brain is full, but you've helped no end in updating knowledge for my notes on farming in Abilene and Dickinson County. I think I'm beginning to get the picture between any old farm operations just hanging on and the newer and bigger ones."

What we did not talk about was any connection to pioneer days or later and ethnicity and farming. I suppose I could go to the phone book or just out to the cemeteries and gravestones (like I did for "Rural Odyssey II") or yet just recall names of farmers at church, or kids of farmers I knew. It had been quite a few years now, ten to be exact since those high school days, but it was all German, Irish, Scotch, Swedish, Russian and the like, and more Scandinavian. I do not know who got to the river bottom first, but it had to be the Germans, and the Catholic Germans at that, and maybe in the 1920s or teens of the 1900s. My Dad's batch of Irish farmers were still up in SE Nebraska until his dad died and his Mom moved the brood down to farm country north of Abilene in the 1920s. I think I'll just leave it at that for now.

But we did get into a politics a bit and that was of course related to economics and Abilene. Ron said since I had left and gone to college, and even in the days we were up at the Juco and certainly now there were big debates going on in Abilene.

"One was whether to try to bring in manufacturing jobs to provide work for kids, including farm kids, that could not make it on the farms. The town even established that commercial zone out northwest and west of the fairgrounds. So far there is just one taker, Russel Stover Candy Company. The logical choice would be maybe making farm equipment. But ideas are few and any prospective companies want "freebies" to even talk – tax breaks or incentives, free land, and utilities. The town just does not have the budget to do it.

"There always have been people in town as well who thought we farmers were getting 'a free ride.' Government crop subsidies, loans for storage bins for wheat and silos for silage, discounts on gasoline for tractors, that sort of thing, have always been debated. The general argument is if the farmers get it, why don't small business merchants? And it's a good argument. All I can say it has kept a lot of marginal operations going and has helped us for sure.

"You know Kansas is Republican, has been for as long as I can remember, at least for local and state offices, and mostly for national. Truman was the first Democrat I can ever remember being elected, and then not until John F. Kennedy and now Lyndon B. Johnson although he came in as vice - president. I think Eisenhower's days did most for us. But it's more than that and more complicated. Farmers are independent cusses, and most don't want the government telling them what to do or interfering in their operations (my Dad said the government ruined the creamery business in Kansas with subsidies to the big dairies). People associate the Democrats with high taxes, big government spending programs, big city politics and interests and "FDR welfare" for folks who don't need it and other shenanigans. Republicans seem to stand for rugged individualists, hard - working independent people who can pull themselves up by their bootstraps, low government spending and low taxes."

I said, "That sure seems to be a contradiction these days. Even Eisenhower in his last speech before he left the presidency warned against the "military – industrial complex," and I don't think anybody knew more about that than he. And his regime put through the Interstate Highway System, all federal money. So I guess it just depends, doesn't it?"

"Yeah, but don't try to run for office in Abilene on a Democratic ticket. Of course, there are exceptions. Sheriff Wiley has been in office for years, so maybe all this talk by us is just hot wind, or better, pissing in the wind."

"Or, on the other hand, preaching to the choir," I said.

10

DECISIONS, DECISIONS

We spent Thanksgiving that Fall with Mariah's family in Overland Park, enjoying a respite from College and Abilene routine. There was nothing really unusual to report about school other than what the reader already knows or for the day to day in Abilene either. What really was on our minds was, uh, us. And the wedding and can I say it, the future. You would think it would be easy, all cut and dried, but not so. Country boy and city girl, Irish American Catholic and Spanish Sephardic Jewish, but both of us basically non practicing. There were two long talks in the Palafox home, one in the kitchen over coffee and another in the living room on Saturday evening before getting up to drive back to Abilene on that Sunday.

The first one, and easier, after much discussion it was decided we would go it alone at the Ph.D. hooding ceremony in mid - January in Boston, with the promise that we would stop at the Palafoxes on the way home to teach Spring Term in Abilene. It was, frankly, a lousy time to be flying back East and the weather being a dicey factor. It would be a red – eye into Boston on a Friday night, lodging at the Inn at the Harvard Club of Boston (arranged on a limited basis for Ph.D. candidates and guests) some sleep at the Inn, the ceremony the next day and a reception – party that night (a Harvard tradition) at the same Harvard Club of Boston! This was when professors and departments pulled rank to reserve space in the huge bar and Veritas dining room for their new PhDs, select invited school chums and mainly the professors themselves. In otherwards, a purely academic blowout! We would have friends take pictures, and both of us anticipated cheery times with the academic crowd. There might be a little sleep before the red eye after midnight back to Kansas City, a night with Benjamin and Ariel (and maybe Josh) and then "home" to Abilene.

The second conversation was a little more difficult. Mariah and I had tentatively set the date for the wedding for June 10th 1970, a Sunday. The dicey part was how it would be and where it would take place. We shared our opinion of having it out on the farm in Abilene. I think Ariel went into shock and Benjamin was not far behind. There must have been a dozen questions (objections, doubts?). "What about our friends and Jewish connections here in Kansas City? Mariah's high school and sorority friends? David, Sarah, Jaime and Lucas in Mexico City? Could we expect all of them to go to a back yard on a farm in Kansas for our only daughter's marriage? And would the ceremony follow Jewish tradition, the rabbi, the outdoor canopy, readings, vows, dinner and reception? There are so many nice places in Kansas City that are expert in doing this."

Ben and Ariel had obviously been thinking about this for some time. But, hey, whose wedding is it? Mariah would consult, but she rules.

In response to Ben and Ariel, I said, "I think, and rightfully so, your thoughts are valid." How is that for filial piety?

But the other side of the coin was not unreasonable (as both Mariah and I tried to stay calm and explain to Benjamin and Ariel): It would not be a Catholic wedding with a mass, but our good friend Father Kramden would officiate in a formal ceremony, but with a Rabbi of Mariah and Palafox choosing at his side. Mariah and I would pick bridesmaids, best men, music, flowers and the like, but always open to Palafox and O'Brien suggestions. We would have the canopy brought from Kansas City, ask Rabbi Hershowitz of Palafox choosing from growing up days (the same who officiated during Mariah's bat mitzvah back in K.U. days), the band providing dinner and dance music, even the catered dinner. The three – hour drive (max) was not a whole lot longer than to cross-town places in the Kansas City area, a "slam dunk" for wedding caterers. We could book ahead of time almost the entire three floors of the new Express Holiday Inn Motel north of town, room for all the Palafoxes and friends and other out of towners. My family, a few relatives, old friends, our joint friends from Abilene (remember we are now in our fourth year if you count the original junior college days) and of course new friends from the College. I'm thinking of all the names the reader has already met in both "Rural Odyssey II" and now in this narrative.

Mariah's "bachelorette" party including friends from Kansas City and K.U. could be at the rented Country Club, my "bachelor's party" at the same place a night later? Or, more likely, the bar and card room at the Elks' Club.

11

A SURPRISE CALL AND REVELATIONS – BUSINESSES IN ABILENE

We left it all "on the table" with Ben and Ariel, only to be resolved just a month later (time going by, necessarily so) aided by an unexpected happening and bit of news from Abilene. It was a phone call and request to go for a drink and dinner to Mr. and Mrs. Cline's house, one of the nicer Victorians out on West 3rd street in town. We did not know either of them on a social basis, but I had bought a new suit and some Levis in the clothing store. Mr. Cline said they knew my family, of course on a casual basis, from years in Abilene, knew Dad from the Elks Club and knew both of us from our work at the Juco, and my part in foiling that bombing at the Eisenhower Museum back in 1966. They had long thought of calling us but now seemed to be the right time. And the word was around town I was messing with a "History of Abilene" and Mr. Cline said he thought he could help with that. How he knew? I'm sure from Wally Galatin.

We went over on a Saturday evening in early December. Bill and Jenni Cline received us warmly and when we went into the living room there was a second couple, the Schwartz's of the Ladies' Apparel Shop in Abilene. Both couples were older, my parents' generation, but seemed happy to meet the "young folks." After some chitchat when I said I could remember Mom first, then Caitlin, shopping in the ladies' apparel store probably from the late 1940s, and my older brothers Paul and Joe O'Brien in the Cline's Men's Store sporadically during the 1950s.

I said, "Pardon me, but most of the farmers in town probably did most of the clothes and shoe shopping at J.C Penney's or the old RHV stores. My memories are at Penney's with the Dickies Jeans and that old electric cash box system up to the second floor." Our hosts all laughed heartily saying they wish it were still around for history's sake.

I asked about the stores and their families, when they came to Abilene and how they got started. Paul refreshed his drink and became enthused to say, "Mike and Mariah, there is much history to all this. Do you know the term 'haberdashery'? (I said I did, recalling President Truman worked in one in Kansas City, Missouri before going into politics. Our hosts all remembered that.) It is an old term for a store selling men's clothing, specifically, suits, shirts and neckties. But in the old days the store would sell as well sewing supplies, buttons, zippers and the like. You know in our store we provide with the cost of the article free alternation, almost always on fine suit trousers. Well, the Cline store, my brother and I, are from that tradition, and it includes way back the skill of the local tailor. What's the song, "Tinker, tailor, Soldier, Sailor"? It's an old, old nursery rhyme used for counting buttons! Not many folks know that.

"How we ended here is really not a mystery but not a bit likely, since Abilene is such a small town. Our parents had a small store in Kansas City and another in Wichita in the boom days of the 1920s. They did well and the family wanted to branch out; Dad did his research and concluded Abilene would be the best possible location, first of all, no real competition but also potentially a good market. Churches and church people are our best customers. And not just in town but the surrounding area. No respectable gentleman in those days and until recently would go to church services without dressing in suit, possibly vest, long sleeve white shirt, tie and a Fedora! We provided them all, along with fine dress shoes, and that tailoring service and became Abilene's premier men's store."

Jan Swartz spoke up, saying, "And we have almost an identical story for ladies' apparel – the nice dresses and hats and even parasols for Sunday church."

Her husband Howard added, "And don't forget weddings, anniversaries, and even high school graduations. We are good friends and have an informal arrangement with Wally Galatin and previously with his father at the photo studio. Wally's Dad would send us the names of all the folks needing photographs for such occasions and send them to our stores to get "fixed up" for the photos (at a suggested small fee, a percentage, as usual). Mike and Mariah, that's the way business works."

But all this leads to my main point. What we are telling you is in the strictest confidence. Mariah, it is known among a small group of people in town that you are ethnically Jewish, Sephardi I may add. And that you have done marvelous work both in your early years at the Juco three years ago and now at the college. And also that you and Mike are to be married soon. We know of your study at Brown and Harvard and as you know there is a strong link to our tradition as well there. We thought it was about time for you to meet some new friends who share your heritage and want to give you a very long overdue "welcome back" and encourage you to make your lives here.

"But there is a proviso: for many reasons, we do not talk of our ethnic roots and in fact are upstanding members of the local Methodist Church. Do not be shocked! Mariah, it is no different than the generations of your Sephardi ancestors who became out of necessity "conversos" to survive in Spain and then elsewhere in Spanish or Portuguese dominions. You know that New Amsterdam draws from the Jewish migrants from Europe but also the Caribbean and earlier from Brazil. In Abilene it turns out to be quite a workable and pleasant arrangement. Both the Swartzes and us are members of the Chamber of Commerce and Rotary Club as well. We have never experienced any difficulty in Abilene, nor will you. Mariah, we just wanted to provide you a 'home away from home' should you wish to talk of our commonality."

It was Mariah's turn. She graciously thanked them and said it would be fun and interesting to meet again to socialize. She laughed and said, "There is one small problem. My parents in Kansas City are a bit reticent about their only daughter getting married in a farm town and worse, on a farm in the middle of nowhere. (Mariah filled them in on wedding plans, including canopy, priest and rabbi, music and the rest.)"

Jenni spoke up, "Mariah if I may be so bold. If you allow me, I will be glad to telephone your parents, introduce ourselves, share how proud and happy we are to have you here, and best of all marrying a town favorite and hero (from the Eisenhower Center). And how this 'country wedding' can have all the trappings of those social halls in Kansas City and more! The Schmidt farm is gorgeous (we can tell from just driving by from Highway 40) and I think your wedding will indeed top the social calendar for many come June and be long remembered."

12

APPROVAL AND MORE REVELATIONS

Mariah said she would let them know, but after we talked it over a day or two, we decided the call might be a good idea. Jumping ahead a bit, it all happened just the next week and then both Ben and Ariel got on the line to us with their approval and renewed enthusiasm and anxious to start the planning. (We think the Jewish connection and Jenni's "silver tongue" and good words did the trick.) Planning became complicated like weddings, but between us, Benjamin and Ariel, David and Sarah in Mexico City, and Mariah's brothers and brothers – in - law, Ron and Caitlin, and all kinds of hints and help from the Clines and the Swartzes (all behind the scenes) the wheels were set in motion for that next June and the big day. Details as they come.

However, the rest of that delightful Saturday evening visit and a time or two later was an insiders' "scoop" on the history of commerce in Abilene and more than enough details for my notes perhaps to be written up later. Funny, but the research I had done for "Rural Odyssey II" turned out to have a good deal of the story which our hosts chipped in to tell. The earliest days of Timothy and Eliza Hersey in 1857 and their store to supply the Butterfield Overland Stage Line west of Mud Creek, then the halcyon cattle days of cattle baron Joseph McCoy with drives from Texas, the railhead with the Kansas Pacific and the Drover's Cottage Hotel. All were among the things I had written of earlier on.

The Clines and the Swartz's talked of the whole amazing saga of businessman and inventor C. L. Brown all the way from 1902 to his bankruptcy in 1935 - a real "businessman and tycoon" who started with a grist mill south of the river, then developed Abilene's infra-structure of power lines and telephones as well as the classy Sunflower Hotel and the first major investment company the United Trust. At the same time true retailing took place with A.L. Duckwall from 1901 to 1937 who brought the Five and Dime Store to Abilene, starting with a bicycle shop across the street and ended with no less than thirty stores before he was done. I had wonderful childhood memories of the store, everything from the candy counter, to the cowboy toys of Roy Rogers or Gene Autry cap guns and holsters and even a Red Ryder B – B Gun. And, oh yeah, the 35 cent lunch of a toasted cheese sandwich, a pickle and mashed potatoes with brother Joe and sister Caitlin for a once a week treat. And of course, the Seelye Mansion with the patent medicine trade or as some called it "snake oil" of Mr. Seelye who sold his many medicines via cart and buggy all over the plains and west to Denver.

I won't repeat all the details here (it's all in "Rural Odyssey II"). But our hosts knew them all. The change from cattle to farming came mainly because of the Homestead Act, the religious tone of the town from the first settlers from River Brethren roots in Pennsylvania and then more farmers who were mainly Protestants. Only at the beginnings of the 20th century came the wave of immigration from Europe and the Catholic Germans and Irish. Streets were paved, sidewalks built, a big city park came, and as I wrote before, no less than twenty – seven churches. Schools in the 20th century were named, gulp, after assassinated Presidents with Lincoln, Garfield and McKinley in succession. And from Wild Bill Hickock we now had "good ole' Sheriff Wiley" and a respectable police force and fire department.

Bill and Howard, Jenni and Jan either knew or knew of most of the people who ran businesses from the 1930s on and many from my growing up times. They talked of the Old Court House south of the Union Pacific tracks, just west of the Belle Springs Creamery and Ice Plant (where Ike Eisenhower and his Dad both worked, and where I used the same ice tongs working in the summers after high school) which used to be McCoy's Drover's Cottage, a hotel for cowboys, the Citizens' Bank, the First Abilene National Bank and the local businesses like the Shockey and Landes building, the big RHV corner with the four stores run by four brothers, the Toothpick Building with the tin roof, ceiling fans and barber shop with spittoons. What am I leaving out? The United Trust Building, the Sunflower Hotel, the A & P Grocery Store, J.C. Penney's, barber shops, drug stores, the whole kit and kaboodle. And they knew all the proprietors, colleagues in the Chamber of Commerce and Rotary. And the doctors and lawyers, many from Dad's days and my own.

Talk came around to the beauty of Abilene, no accident. City planning with the grid of numbered east-west and named north-south streets. The planting of all the Oak, Elm and other wonderful shade trees, many now over 100 years old, and of course all the old mansions and Victorians. The Seelye Mansion, the Kirby Mansion and the historic Lebold Mansion were on their list. And Jan remembered the long history of the public library and how William Jennings Bryan gave a speech and donated funds to help get it started.

Wow. And of course, the big one, the Eisenhower name was primary and foremost. Both families were familiar with the history of the three major rail lines since the goods and products for their stores were shipped in primarily from Kansas City and Chicago in the East and from the Levi Company in San Francisco from the West. That is until the end of World War II when trucking became prevalent and more efficient than the old rail lines, with National Highway 40 running right through town, from Kansas City in the East to Denver on west.

Like I say, I really detailed most of this in "Rural Odyssey II" and am just talking about it now because of what our new friends told us. I think the reader gets the idea – Abilene is one historic place for being so small and "in the middle of nowhere" as maybe they used to say in 1869. But not now. Just see the traffic on the Interstate north of town.

The Clines' and Swartz's Abilene Photo Gallery

The Seeyle Mansion

Main Street, Abilene

The Old Sunflower Hotel

Union Pacific Station

13

CHRISTMAS, END OF TERM AND BOSTON

When you think of it, maybe no big deal, but it was our last "unmarried" Christmas in Abilene. We had two weeks before January when fall term would finish with exams and a flourish. And then, our quick trip to Boston. The weather was cold, but no big snowstorms until just two or three inches on Christmas Eve. We had dinner that evening with Mom and Dad, opened presents, did a toast or two and then left them until coming by next morning for a trip down to St. Andrew's and mass. But later on Christmas Eve there was sort of a "command performance," a party up at Dr. Halderson's house. The latter was a happy occasion with most of our friends from the College, too much Christmas candy (oh, did I say I hate fruit cake), but wine and bar drinks if you chose. Everyone was reminiscing over events from the Fall term, and in private, asking many questions about you know what the next June. And Dr. Halderson and his wife joined in, toasting the soon – to – be Mr. and Mrs. O'Brien. Oh, Mariah had announced she would do a legal name change with two official names as in the Hispanic tradition, ergo, Mariah O'Brien de Palafox. She said I could call her "Señora Mariah O'Brien" on a formal basis. Ha.

On Christmas Day after Mass we returned to the apartment and had some quiet time, really our first Christmas together. I made Irish Coffees, we talked and had a nap before picking up Mom and Dad and going out to Ron and Caitlin's for the big Christmas Dinner. It was as expected – chaos - the four children hyped with too much Christmas Candy, wanting to show us their new presents and play with them. I think the grandparents were better at that than us. There was pleasant talk of school, the kids' goings-on, who was who at mass, Father Kramer's excellent voice in singing the High Mass, and finally talk of the coming months and the wedding. We had tentatively accepted Ron and Caitlin's offer for the wedding, the whole thing, lock, stock and barrel, given them the date, and said nothing would be nailed down until we would have a whole lot more specifics after this next week with Ben and Ariel in Kansas City. Did they want to back out? "No way! I think we can top anything like this ever done in Abilene. Mariah, we guarantee you will be proud of the place and your decision." She smiled, was a bit quiet for her, and said, "I think you can see I'm concerned with the 'country wedding' plan, just not totally sure. We have not been down this road before. They will be talking about this in the big city; we're breaking new ground – a country Irish – Jewish wedding - or is that something you farmers would say?"

Taking a tired Mom and Dad home, and us not much less weary, we packed that evening for the car trip to Kansas City the next day. Roads were icy, but the Interstate pavement had mostly cleared by mid-morning when we left.

Then there was a delightful but eventful visit in Overland Park. Lots to talk about. End of term, Boston but mainly the wedding. All in due course.

14

WHAT IS TO COME - SPRING TERM IN ABILENE 1970

January rolled around with classes and cold weather. Before I go on to other stuff there is some unfinished business to talk about. Once spring semester began, Jeremiah Watson's music class itself started out small, but manageable, about ten kids from the College. The first hour was for introduction to music and music theory. Jeremiah was a whiz at that and most of all patient. There was the cliché – "You white folks don't seem to have much rhythm! Let's work on the counting." We all laughed, and I said, "The old saying is 'We can't walk and chew gum at the same time.' I don't think I can dance with Dentyne in my mouth either." We learned of treble clef and base clef, the octatonic and pentatonic scales, 2/4-time, 4/4 time, and 3/3 Waltz time. Jeremiah kept it simple, at least in the beginning. Because he knew I played the guitar and remembered our singing of pop and some country tunes, he said, "This next class is on the key of C, the only one you need for Ricky Nelson or Johnny Cash. Elvis liked the E key and so did Hank Williams, but they all had 8 notes. Almost all pop music is simple like that. Little Ricard and Chuck Berry started off with three chords as well. Now, if you want to get serious, we'll do a class on Blues some morning."

The second hour was the fun time. The singing. We did the late fifties and early sixties pop songs, after all that was what Jeremiah, I, and Mariah knew. The college kids of course thought they were old fashioned and out of date but seemed to get into "the oldies." On select occasions, the Ebenezer Choir would show up, and we worked on "church" songs and Spirituals.

Word must have gotten around; more and more college kids showed up by the end of January and enthusiastically joined the group (maybe to meet other kids, guys or chicks). Jumping ahead, after that one month of January, at my and Mariah's insistence Jeremiah got his Dad's permission to have a "concert" or performance or whatever you wanted to call it, on a Friday night at the church. Saturday night was regular service so that was out. And we all agreed it would be open to the public for donations. I'm not kidding you, the church was packed, mainly the college kids' friends, but also some teachers from the school, relatives, and one felicitous guest, William Donaldson from the "Reflector Chronicle" (he admitted it was his first time in the church). The Ebenezer First Gospel Church is small, so that meant maybe 120 people. They were tapping their toes, dancing in the pews, in the aisle and encouraged to join in on the tunes they knew. Most were swaying to "Will the Circle Be Unbroken," "Swing Low Sweet Chariot," and a dazzling finale of "Amazing Grace" with singers from the church choir, Jeremiah and me with guitar accompaniment, and then Jeremiah with a haunting trumpet solo of the melody to close the performance. No ones' eyes were dry. A standing ovation! And "When's the next concert?" Reverend and Mrs. Watson were introduced as our hosts and were thanked at the beginning and the end, and reminding that all were welcome the next night for regular services.

Tears almost come to my eyes telling all this. Our Saturday classes and the concert probably did more for race relations in Abilene than anything in past town history. And that was not even on our minds. One other reason was William Donaldson put news of the concert with photos on the front page of the "Chronicle" the next day, Saturday. We do not know who, but there were some very generous and appreciative folks that night.

$350 dollars were collected, and we, the group, unanimously voted to put it toward the purchase of a small electric organ for the church. When contacted later, the owner of the only music store in town said he knew of a used one that we might be able to get, and for a good price. It turned out that two months later an anonymous donor mailed a $1000 check to Reverend Watson "For the Purchase of Your Electric Organ" and it all became reality.

And Dr. Halderson and his wife were there that first night, glowing at the results. He would tell Jeremiah, me, and Mariah, that Jeremiah's class would get extra billing in the Spring College newspaper.

15

BOSTON - IN THE "HOOD"

Back to early January and after Jeremiah's classes, next on the agenda was the big trip back to Boston. A couple of things to keep in mind: first, the "hooding" was required by Harvard, no "hooding," no official degree. (I'm talking about academic regalia: the long affair that goes over your head and then hangs down your back, with color determined not only by your university, but your college and department. A long black academic gown goes along with it and the mortar board top hat. Just kidding. It is square, but diamond shaped and facing the front, flat with a tassel. ("Mariah, it's like the surrey with the fringe on top." "Mike, I've seen mortar boards and tassels since you were in short pants.") Okay. Secondly, this was no small thing, and I don't want to make light of it. How many families have one Harvard graduate much less two? And at the same time? Because we finished the degrees officially at the end of the summer school calendar of 1969, theoretically we should have attended graduation ceremonies in May of 1970. Our end of Fall Semester ceremony was new, an experiment to fulfill the requirement but without all the official falderal (and I suspect to lessen the size and complications of the huge ceremony in May). Thus, the Harvard Club and all that.

So we flew the red – eye into Logan, freezing cold but no rain or snow, splurged on a cab directly to the Harvard Club and Harvard Inn. Our rather modest and even spartan lodging was waiting, so we checked in and slept for about three hours before the festivities started. There was a noon luncheon in old, traditional Harvard Hall where we sat with our advisors, chosen faculty (they may have been invited to attend as a "command performance," i.e. "It's part of your job.") and colleagues graduating, all of us in the same boat. Dr. Skidmore was there, smiling and happy to greet me, "How are things in the great outback?" Over a drink, I filled him in saying I was very happy with my decision, at least thus far. "So you are on deck at DDEC? Well, that's something (but I could tell he still thought I should have been on to greater things). Maybe we'll get you out of there in a year or two and move on up to better things! I doubt there is much pressure to publish, but do you have anything in the till?"

"Tom, I've got a tentative agreement with Dr. Agustín Yañez for the dissertation, a book he will back through the Mexican Ministry of Education. That's for openers. And I'm working on that history of Abilene."

"Fine, fine, don't forget your roots, modest as they might be. (Ha ha.) I could use a bit of that influence in Mexico myself. However, I'm sidetracked in Brazil right now and will be for the near future, a follow – up on the 1965 book. But, where's Mariah? I haven't seen her."

"She's off with the English Crowd at the other end of the hall, but we are hoping you and I, she and her advisor Dr. Cromwell can join us for the cocktails and dinner at Veritas this evening."

"Este es el plan mi hijo. ["That's the plan my boy."] And your department co-grads will be there as well. We advisors wear more than one hat, so I've got to be equally fair to the four of you. Let's see, if you all buy me drinks, then you can get a pool going for the taxi ride home. I wouldn't miss it my boy; that's the fun part. But let's get that contraption over your head first."

There was a lengthy affair that afternoon in the great hall with all the Liberal Arts' programs included, including of course English and Latin American Studies. Dr. Skidmore had arranged, as per custom, one of the department secretaries to get photos of the actual hooding, and since she knew Mariah well, accomplished the same thing for her. It got a bit noisy and rowdy, and a few rules were bent, but I just remember giving Mariah a huge kiss and hug as she came down from the stage. "Mariah, I am so proud and humbled to be in your presence and happy for us both." She was in tears, but all smiles, and said, 'Ole' goy and favorite mensch and love of my life, the feeling is entirely mutual. Doctor y Doctora!"

What started out as sedate turned a bit, what shall we say, noisy. Cocktails in the Veritas Lounge, all of us reminiscing over the last two or three years. I do not believe it became maudlin, but at least sentimental. However you think, there is a bond established – Harvard Ph.D. - and although I doubted we would ever see much of our co – graduates, the "deal was sealed." Good times were remembered, classes and professors and some good and bad jokes recalled, maybe some differences settled, like grade envy or such. The cocktails melded into a fine dinner in the dining room with more toasts, good food, then abrazos, hugs and kisses and fond goodbyes. Professors even known to be rivals parted in cheery company, and, well, that was that. Tom Skidmore said, "Stay in touch and see if you can leave that 'sertão' [backland] and make it down to Brazil." Mariah and I gladly eased on out of the restaurant, packed our bags and our diplomas and took the taxi to Logan.

On the way home on the plane, we did a lot of reminiscing after a couple of drinks of scotch on my part and wine on hers. How we met up at the Juco in the fall of 1963, both young and rookie teachers, how we began dating, got along so well, and then nervously introduced each other to respective families, and then the beginning of our travels in life together, Mexico in 1964 and Spain in 1965. We each recalled the meeting of the respective parents, times during holidays, and then all culminating in that turbulent year of trouble in Abilene in 1965 -1966.

We recalled the mutual decision to leave the juco and Abilene in 1966 and do what we always wanted, study for advanced degrees. My year at Brown, hers in Law at Harvard, both of us at Harvard for two more years (to 1969), back to Mexico, and the return to Abilene. And now! Whew! Harvard seemed long ago and Abilene full of life.

16

END OF TERM AND FLURRY OF ACTIVITY

We were both exhausted to get into Kansas City, but excited to tell Ben and Ariel the details and show them the diplomas. Same thing in Abilene.

Back in the groove at the College we were both happy to be doing what we knew, teaching and advising. Enrollment was staying steady in second term, nothing new to report. Dr. Halderson did call us in in early February to "make good on that promise." Uh oh, what promise? "We at DDEC are always on the lookout for more students and like I told you before you returned, we need to do some active recruiting. That's where you and Mariah come in, what better 'upcoming young faculty at DDEC' could there be? I'd like you to take a Friday or three and visit some high schools to see if we can stir up excitement for them to at least visit here. I'm thinking the larger population centers, Dodge City and Garden City out west, and one or two smaller towns like Ellsworth and maybe Newton. I'm leaving out the areas closer to the big colleges and even Kansas City schools. It would be like three years ago, Friday visits to English and History classes, maybe Spanish as well, give a spiel about DDEC and see what happens. I know both of you are busy, but I'm just thinking of three visits. You could do Ellsworth and Newton on a day each, and maybe a three-day trip out west to Garden City and Dodge City. I'll get someone to cover for your classes, particularly on that one long foray."

We both suggested that it be in March because, frankly, April and May toward the end of term would be busy, plus our wedding preparations might preclude the extra travel. Doc Halderson agreed saying it was just a "trial balloon" to see how things might work for the future.

So that is what happened. It took up all the spare time in March. We did Newton in one day, visited the high school and I went to history and Spanish classes and Mariah to English. The kids all knew about DDEC but were full of questions about Harvard (that's how Dr. Halderson had introduced us via phone calls). Our answer: if you come to Abilene first and do well, there's no limit what you can do later. I won't deny it – we took time to visit the old historic train station and the famous Harvey House Restaurant, famous for the girls Harvey recruited just to waitress his restaurants all along the train cities out west in the teens of the 20th century. Ellsworth was put off until a later date, mainly because we were running out of time that Spring.

The Garden City and Dodge City excursion I'll call it was much the same touting the name and opportunities at DDEC. We did one each day, visiting classes and touting DDEC. And there was a bit of tourism afterwards. We were both impressed by the huge feedlots in both Garden City and Dodge City, but I thought Boot Hill was hokey and playing on Abilene's fame. Well, the locals probably would not have agreed, but mission accomplished. Several letters of application came in to DDEC the following weeks.

It was then, late March, that we had an event reminiscent of those bad days of 1965 and 1966, but for altogether different reasons. It shook us both up, maybe more for me for than Mariah because it was I who had first pushed the return to Abilene. We woke one morning, showered, ate breakfast, and walked out the door to respective cars to go up to school (we were on different schedules and needed both cars). The sight that greeted us was both cars, front and back door and top of the trunk were painted with red Swastikas, and in sprawling uneven letters, 'We don't cotton to no Jews or Jew lovers in Abilene." I ran back in and called Sheriff Wiley who answered right away. "Wiley, it's Mike. It's happened again but it's worse." I told him of the swastikas and message, he said to sit tight, don't touch either car (fingerprints?), go back in the house and he would soon be there in an unmarked county car. In about ten minutes he pulled up, walked slowly to the side door of the house and we were both looking out the window so saw him come.

He shook my hand and patted Mariah on the shoulder saying, "This time I know damned well who's behind this. We've got some young punks in town, skinheads I think they call 'em these days, neo-Nazis, many admire Hitler, want only the white race to rule, an Aryan supremacy. Every few months they do some painting, but this time it was your cars."

Mariah said, "How did they know about us, about me? We've been so low – key about it all."

"Mariah, it's a small town, full of gossip and some punks who don't have anything better to do. They are connected to shitheads just like them over in Junction City and Salina. We are in touch with the KBI who are apprised of it all and keep a watch out. The punks could have heard about you from any number of folks or ways, an inadvertent remark at a football game, at a picnic, hell, I don't know. Or maybe they saw you parked at Reverend Watson's church, that's one of their targets. Mike's lived here most of his life, and everyone in town knows he is back at the College and some know that you two are engaged, and I daresay that you are ethnically a Jew from the big city. Hey, I want you to throw something over the cars, old bed sheets, whatever, and I'll get a tow truck out here this morning with something to keep them covered and get them down to the paint shop on Spruce. Joey Walsh is a magician and can take that red paint off, do some sanding and repaint your cars in three days' time. Maybe you can walk up to work today, just tell folks some punks keyed your cars. Call your insurance company and get a couple of loaners. These jerks have been caught once before, taken to juvenile court and fined, but this time ole Judge Rasher won't be so damned lenient."

We followed orders and walked up and back to school that day, and the insurance company contacted the Chevy dealership and they drove out two cars that afternoon. The Walsh Body Shop got hot on our cars and Wiley was good to his word; they were back in three days. The weight of the law turned out to come true as well. Wiley was right; it was three young punks with earrings out of their ears, nose and lips who were hauled into court the next morning. Second offense. The assholes still had the red paint cans in an old tin can pile back of their rundown apartment south of the Rock Island tracks, not far from where the old hobo camp used to be. I'm not sure what Wiley told them, or how he may have "encouraged" cooperation, but they admitted the crime. Judge Rasher was in no mood for leniency and sent them all out to Larned to the Juvenile Prison for six months. And he added a warning that if anything happened again, or even if Abilene were "tainted by their smell," it would be ten years in Lansing, the state prison. We were assured by both the judge and Wiley that it was a sporadic incident, that it was nothing personal on the part of the delinquents, just less than intelligent vandalism on their part.

That was easy for them to say; it was a helluva lot more difficult to deal with Mariah's state of mind. All the above, I mean the apprehension of the culprits, court date and sentencing, had happened on the first week of April. The wedding was just two months away. As the reader knows, Mariah is one tough lady and not about to turn her back on a fight, nor is Benjamin in Kansas City. We drove down to Overland Park the next weekend, to talk about wedding planning, but also to deal with what happened with our cars.

Benjamin was shocked and not shocked. "Kids, you know well enough this can happen anywhere, anytime. Look at what happened here in the city last year at the practice and the ones of my friends and colleagues. I am surprised the little farm town like Abilene would have anything like it, but extremism and pardon me, ignorance and stupidity, are not just big city things. Mike, you know Mariah dealt with anti – Semitism at the sorority in college, but that was secret, all hush – hush. Those bastard kids in Abilene should indeed be taught a lesson, but I doubt that a juvenile detention center has classes on how to alleviate anti – Semitism. I do have confidence in your law enforcement people; we have the KKK and Eisenhower business and the aftermath as proof. Mariah, Mike, you just be smart and get on with life. Let's go down to the old Deli in the Plaza, have our usual treat and come home and talk about this, what do you call it, 'shindig' you are planning out in Abilene.

The talk that p.m. was long, a bit detailed with lots of exchanges of ideas, or not, and here's the gist of it. The wedding would be outside on the manicured farm lawn, Ron would arrange for tables and chairs (from the Knights of Columbus Hall at St. Andrew's), that is, once we gave him the number for the guests. All table decorations would come from a big shop in Kansas City provided by the Palafoxes with Ariel in charge. This was a chance to see just one of her many organizational talents. The shop specialized in Jewish weddings, so they arranged for the wedding canopy and such as well. We discussed the menu and made decisions based on favorites of both families, but an interesting Jewish dessert custom (and a favorite of mine), no less than Lemon Merengue Pie for all!

David would handle all the refreshments including fine champagne and wine, but the caterer would bring it, the glasses, and the two special wine glasses wrapped in napkins to be broken after the wedding vows were said (in remembrance of the destruction of the temple in Jerusalem, a reminder of pain and loss of the Jewish people and a world in need of healing), but also "As these glasses shatter, so may our marriage never break". Ron would handle the iced down beer. Chicken, beef, or salmon would be offered to each guest (although Ariel estimated the latter would be mainly for the Jewish group). And as mentioned, once again, because it happened to be one of my favorites and also Jewish custom, Lemon Merengue Pie for dessert, a huge order, but Ariel said the caterer could handle it and the merengue would be the best!

The Palafoxes understand the parameters of the wedding ceremony. Father Kramer would preside and present the wedding vows. But Rabbi Hershowitz of the Reformed Judaism Synagogue in Kansas City would stand to his side and repeat a short Reformed Jewish version of the vows. However, Mariah and I had written our own and that would be the main thrust of the ceremony.

Ah, the best part – the reception dinner, music, and lots of dancing. A small quartet of musicians from Kansas City would be in charge and could do it all – pop, old timey, country and yes, Irish and Jewish!

So, that's the main thing for now. Mariah, I and her Mom (with Ben's input) made up a tentative wedding invitation list, soon to be mailed out yet in early April) It included the Palafoxes of Overland Park, a few select friends there, the Palafoxes of Mexico City, three or four of Mariah's KU sorority friends, the advisors of dissertations (a formality; we did not really think they would come). From Abilene, my family of course, and friends from the College and many of the people in this narrative. I think it came out close to one hundred by the time we were done.

Ariel said the main thing is to get the rabbi and priest on the calendar, then the catering company, and then write up and send the invitations. Mariah and I would handle Abilene needs and she and David would do Kansas City.

So it went in hurry up time, all done by the end of the 4th week of April; late in some persons' minds, but a full six weeks before the day! So it was back to the College, busy times with end of term approaching, just normal day to day. That is except the Kent State Massacre in May. Time flew by, lots of phone calls to Ariel and things were falling into place. We did indeed finish classes, said goodbye to the graduates, made tentative plans for the fall term, no big changes on the horizon. Other than the big event.

17

A FEEL - GOOD STORY!

We lucked out – the weather! June 10th can be hot and muggy in the Kansas plains; it wasn't. We hit a cool spell, unseasonably cool in fact, with temperatures in the mid – 70s, a few clouds, like someone was watching over us. Out of towners came in a day or two early and partied up at the Express Hotel north of town. The Palafoxes in two days early did tourism with me and Mariah showing David and Sarah, Jaime and Raquel and Lucas around town. It was a bit like a year or two earlier with Benjamin and Ariel, and they were around to provide editorial comments. The Eisenhower Center, the historic train stations and old Victorians and a big dinner at the famous fried chicken place north of town. It was a big crowd, but they managed a long table with locals (the O'Briens on one side, the Palafoxes on another), and assorted others.

Abilene has that "byob" rule, but brothers Joe and Paul (so long absent from this narrative due to careers in the Navy in the Pacific and dam construction in the Northwest) took care of that with wine and champagne from the local liquor store (Jerry the owner told me that was his best sales day in years). All was very congenial, and I think a lot of "mental stretching" for Sephardi folks from Kansas City and Chicago (two of Benjamin's medical school chums) and Mexico City. Mariah sat with her parents, me with Mom and Dad directly opposite, and we fielded questions and heard jokes about this cowboy town, but all in good sport. Lots of reminiscing of Mexico City, and even Spain along with local stories. It was a somewhat early evening because Ron and Caitlin and the Palafoxes all had to be on hand for the huge next day – setting up the tents, tables and chairs, supervising decoration of tables, and working with the catering team preparing the wedding canopy. Mariah and I were there of course, she directing traffic along with Ariel and Caitlin, me walking the out of towners around the farm with a proud Ron leading the way. I gave Mariah a huge kiss and hug that afternoon and said something inane like "Guess I'll see you tomorrow." She said, "I hope you recognize me in the get – up!"

It was, ahem, girls' night out as planned at the country club, Mariah, her sorority friends, Ariel and Sarah, Wendy from the College, and Caitlin just for the dinner (too much to do yet at home, and the kids all hyper for the event).

The men (Mariah said, "I would like your party more") made a night of it down at the Elks' Club. The liquor did flow, including shots of tequila "a la Mexicana" and with some folks playing poker. Jaime taught us all "póker a la mesa" which turns out to be Five Card Stud Mexican style. And there were the traditional toasts from hometown buddies, my friends who made it from college days, and several Sephardi toasts. All were not presentable in mixed company, if you know what I mean. I was really having a good time when conservative Lucas suggested we call it a night to be quite alert on the big day. It was home to bed in the apartment but Mariah safe and sound (supposedly) with the girl friends in a suite up at the hotel.

That next day was indeed like no other Abilene had ever seen. All the guests arrived on time, flowers were everywhere, the canopy in place, and the band in formal attire but with concert instruments, playing beautiful classical music and old Sephardi wedding songs. We (Mariah and I) had gone against the current a bit by insisting that nice suits and tie would be men's' attire (as opposed to tuxedos), but her three bridesmaids in some pretty snazzy and may I say classy matching long sheath (is that the word?) gowns. We had asked Ron and Caitlin if they wanted to be involved but they graciously said it was enough to handle the "round up" and dinner.

So, on that glorious morning at 11:00 a.m. Father Kramer and Rabbi Hershowitz took their places, Caitlin's youngest served as flower girls, and Benjamin walked a vision of loveliness down the aisle to meet me. He had moist eyes as he put her arm in mine after a kiss on her cheek. They say you do not remember most of your own wedding, but I think we remembered it all. Father Kramer took us through the vows, "Do you Michael O 'Brien and you Mariah Palafox … until death do you part? … Rabbi Hershowitz repeated them in song, a fine cantor he must have been in his youth, in no less than the flowery Sephardi language of Ladino. Jeremiah Watson handed me one ring, Raquel de León the other to Mariah, and we placed them on each other's third finger left hand. Then <u>the kiss </u>and a surprise from behind us – a beautiful chorus of violins and trumpets from one of Kansas City's best Mariachi Bands – a surprise gift from Ben and Ariel, David and Sarah – playing the Mexican Wedding March! Mariah kissed me, hugged me and I thought we would both collapse in each other's arms.

At that point Josh, Jaime and Lucas came forth with the two champagne glasses which we were invited to ceremoniously and hopefully jointly, step on and smash to pieces. A Sephardi custom – "As These Glasses Shatter So May Our Marriage Never Break" - was fulfilled amidst shouts of "Viva Miguel y Mariah" and now more happy music from Mariachi Mexico. We formed a sort of receiving line under the canopy, Mom and Dad, Caitlin and Ron, Joe and Paul on one side, Benjamin and Ariel, David and Sarah, Josh, Jaime, Raquel and Lucas on the other. But now champagne glasses were filled and filled again for all concerned.

Soon thereafter we were all seated, newlyweds at center table with family alongside, and Ben and Ariel's caterers outdid themselves.

Later, during the dinner brother Paul stood up, begged everyone's attention and continued an O'Brien tradition, singing a capella in a deep baritone voice something of a bit of Ireland – "I'll take you home again Kathleen." There was not a dry eye in the crowd especially after he dedicated it with, "Mariah you will always be our Kathleen."

Then came dancing, dining, and celebratory toasts (a bit of one upmanship as usual with the macho guys, friends, brothers and now brothers – in - law). Jeremiah's was among the most memorable: "This wedding is indeed a rebirth of a long friendship, and to these two I owe a rebirth in life." Tears flowed from those of us who knew him well, and his parents Reverend Watson and wife Stella were among them. He asked a special favor: could he play something in honor of the bride and groom. It was a repeat of that night at Ebenezer First Gospel Church, "Amazing Grace."

Benjamin and Ariel later in the afternoon came up to Mariah and me and said, "We had Abilene and your being here all wrong. Shalom. Shalom. So may it be." This might have been in part after they were approached and congratulated by most local folks at the wedding, first all my family, then Dr. Halderson who shook their hands, offered an embrace and said, "Students rave about Mariah. She is so happy; she has found her niche. And Mike is a good man, a good partnership."

That night Mariah and I stayed at our apartment, all planned ahead of time, and a good plan it was. Next day was helping Ron and Caitlin do the cleanup on the lawn, a quick goodbye to Sean and Molly, the drive into Overland Park, a short reunion and goodbye to all the Palafoxes and then the jet and off to a place of dreams – Rio de Janeiro.

EPILOGUE

The Honeymoon ["Luna da Miel"] - Rio de Janeiro, Iguaçú Falls, and Bahia
Mike and Mariah returned to Abilene and DDEC in September 1970.

INTERNET SITES CONSULTED
FOR "RURAL ODYSSEY III"

1. Thomas Skidmore. Wikipedia
2. Charles Wagley. Wikipedia
3. Introduction to Brazil. Charles Wagley
4. Harvard University Buildings. Bing
5. 1964 in the United States. Wiki
6. 1966 in the United States. Wiki
7. Jewish Houses in Newport, Rhode Island.
8. Touro Synagogue. Wiki
9. The Breakers – Newport Mansions.
10. Rhode Island Jewish History.
11. Salve Regina University.
12. Providence College. Wiki
13. Jesuit Colleges in New England. Wiki
14. Ellis Island. History
15. The Staten Island Ferry.
16. New York City in Virtual Walks.
17. Columbus Circle.
18. Map of Boston to New York. Bing
19. Harvard, 1977. Bing
20. Road Map of the U.S.
21. Types of Law Degree at Harvard.
22. School Counselors, Harvard.
23. Dwight D. Eisenhower. Wiki
24. Midwest Old Threshers, Mt. Pleasant, Iowa.
25. Richard Evans Schultes. Wiki
26. What Happened in 1966, Pop Culture.
27. What Happened in 1967, Pop Culture.
28. Institutional Act – 5. Wiki.
29. 20 Essential Jewish Novels.

30. Irish Bars in Boston.
31. Brazilian Bars in Boston.
32. Mexican Bars in Boston.
33. Was 1968 America's Bloodiest Year in Politics.
34. 1980 in the United States. Wiki
35. Santa Fe Trail. Wiki
36. Chamizal Dispute. Wiki
37. King's Chapel, Boston. Wiki
38. Synagogues in Boston.
39. Catholic Cathedrals in Boston.
40. José Guadalupe Posada, Mexico City.
41. The Mexican "Corridos" – Ballads of Adversity and Revolution.
42. Archivo de Corridos en México.
43. Lithography. Wiki.
44. Arsacio Vanegas Arroyo – MFAH.
45. El Teatro Campesino. UCSB Library.
46. Corrido. Wiki.
47. Vicente Mendoza. Bing
48. Brown Digital Repository – Collection.
49. José Guadalupe Posada and the Mexican Broadside.
50. Brady Nikas Collection of Posada Works.
51. Mexican Movement of 1968. Wiki.
52. Secretaría de Educación Pública. México.
53. "Al Filo del Água." Wiki
54. José Guadalupe Posada and Mexican Broadsides.
55. La Catrina.
56. Diego Rivera Murals, Education Ministry.
57. José Guadalupe Posada and Diego Rivera – Fashion – Catrina.
58. José Guadalupe Posada, Hojas Volantes.
59. Posada (José Guadalupe) Collection of Works.
60. The Mexican "Corrido."
61. TSHA "Corridos."

62. The Genesis of Catarina.
63. Museo Mural Diego Rivera. INBA
64. Sueño de una Tarde Dominical en la Alameda Central.
65. JGP. The Skeleton of the People's Editor Antonio Vanegas Arroyo.
66. Posada: mito y mitote, caricatura política.
67. Personajes Históricos de Jalisco – Quién fue Agustín Yañez?
68. Biografía de Agustín Yañez.
69. Agustín Yañez. Wiki
70. Alameda Central.
71. The Sophisticated Mural that Reveals Mexico's History.
72. Murals by Diego Rivera, Palacio de Hernán Cortés, Cuernavaca.
73. History of Morelos.
74. National Action Party (Mexico). Wiki
75. Vicente Fox. Wiki
76. Constitution of Mexico. Wiki
77. La Maestra Rural.
78. The Long Struggle of Mexican Teachers.
79. Soldaderas: The Women of the Mexican Revolution.
80. La Adelita. Lyrics.
81. Corrido de Chihuahua. Lyrics.
82. Gabino Barrera. Lyrics.
83. La Valentina. Lyrics.
84. Los Cuatesones. Corrido del General Francisco Villa.
85. Benjamín Argumedo. Wiki
86. Benito Canales. Lyrics.
87. Corrido de Zenaida. Lyrics.
88. Secretaría de Educación. Portal.
89. The History of Mexico. Wiki
90. Diego Rivera, Jewish.
91. Escuela Nacional Preparatoria. Wiki
92. Villa Meets Zapata – Iconic Photos.
93. José Vasconcelo. Wiki

94. History of Morelos, Conquest and Revolution.

95. The Mural, Memory and Myth of Emiliano Zapata.

96. Agrarian Leader Zapata by Diego Rivera.

97. Historical Events in July 1968.

98. 1968 in the United States.

99. Jewish Wedding Wiki.

100. Food at Jewish Weddings Bing.

101. Estadio Olimpico Universitario – Wiki

102. Mexico's 1968 Massacre: What Really Happened.

103. 1968 Democratic National Convention – Wiki

104. A Year in History – Timeline of 1969 Events.

105. Planning your Jewish wedding in Mexico.

106. Jewish Bachelor Party? – Marriage.

107. Ecumenical and Interfaith Marriages.

108. Food at Jewish Weddings.

109. Mexico 1968 Massacre – What Really Happened.

110. 1968 National Democratic Convention Wiki

111. Jewish Bachelor Party? Marriage.

112. Women of the Wild West: 10 Cowgirls, Outlaws.

113. History of Churches in Abilene, Kansas. Bing

114. Church History.

115. Dickinson County, Kansas.

116. Abilene Heritage Homes Association.

117. Agriculture in Kansas – Kansapedia.

118. Downtown Abilene, Kansas.

119. Abilene Kansas Early History.

120. Best Music Colleges in Kansas.

121. Abilene Kansas Population Statistics.

122. First Presbyterian Church, Abilene, Kansas Wiki.

123. Dwight D. Eisenhower, Wiki.

124. Abilene, Kansas, Wiki.

125. Bale Accumulators.

126. Kansas Peoples: Immigration to Kansas.
127. Central Synagogue, New York – Bing
128. Virtual Tour – Harvard Club of Boston.
129. Abilene, Kansas Business Directory.
130. A Jewish Wedding Tradition Breaking the Glass at a Jewish Wedding.

ABOUT THE AUTHOR

Mark Curran is a retired professor from Arizona State University where he worked from 1968 to 2011. He taught Spanish and Portuguese and their respective cultures. His research specialty was Brazil and its "popular literature in verse" or the "Literatura de Cordel," and he has published many articles in research reviews and now some sixteen books related to the "Cordel" in Brazil, the United States and Spain. Other books done during retirement are of either an autobiographic nature – "The Farm" or "Coming of Age with the Jesuits" - or reflect classes taught at ASU on Luso-Brazilian Civilization, Latin American Civilization or Spanish Civilization. The latter are in the series "Stories I Told My Students:" books on Brazil, Colombia, Guatemala, Mexico, Portugal, and Spain. "Letters from Brazil I, II, and III" is an experiment combining reporting and fiction. "A Professor Takes to the Sea I and II" is a chronicle of a retirement adventure with Lindblad Expeditions - National Geographic Explorer. "Rural Odyssey – Living Can Be Dangerous" is "The Farm" largely made fiction. "A Rural Odyssey II – Abilene – Digging Deeper" is a continuation of "Rural Odyssey." "Around Brazil on the 'International Adventurer' – A Fictional Panegyric" tells of an expedition in better and happier times in Brazil. Next, the author presents a continued expedition in fiction: "Pre – Columbian Mexico – Plans, Pitfalls and Perils." And then, "Portugal and Spain on the 'International Adventurer.'" Now, his latest: "Rural Odyssey III – Dreams Fulfilled and Back to Abilene."

PUBLISHED BOOKS

A Literatura de Cordel. Brasil. 1973

Jorge Amado e a Literatura de Cordel. Brasil. 1981

A Presença de Rodolfo Coelho Cavalcante na Moderna Literatura de Cordel. Brasil. 1987

La Literatura de Cordel – Antología Bilingüe – Español y Portugués. España. 1990

Cuíca de Santo Amaro Poeta-Repórter da Bahia. Brasil. 1991

História do Brasil em Cordel. Brasil. 1998

Cuíca de Santo Amaro – Controvérsia no Cordel. Brasil. 2000

Brazil's Folk-Popular Poetry – "A Literatura de Cordel" – a Bilingual Anthology in English and Portuguese. USA. 2010

The Farm – Growing Up in Abilene, Kansas, in the 1940s and the 1950s. USA. 2010

Retrato do Brasil em Cordel. Brasil. 2011

Coming of Age with the Jesuits. USA. 2012

Peripécias de um Pesquisador "Gringo" no Brasil nos Anos 1960 ou 'A Cata de Cordel" USA. 2012

Adventures of a 'Gringo' Researcher in Brazil in the 1960s or In Search of Cordel. USA. 2012

A Trip to Colombia – Highlights of Its Spanish Colonial Heritage. USA. 2013

Travel, Research and Teaching in Guatemala and Mexico – In Quest of the Pre-Columbian Heritage

    Volume I – Guatemala. 2013
    Volume II – Mexico. USA. 2013

A Portrait of Brazil in the Twentieth Century – The Universe of the "Literatura de Cordel." USA. 2013

Fifty Years of Research on Brazil – A Photographic Journey. USA. 2013

Relembrando - A Velha Literatura de Cordel e a Voz dos Poetas. USA. 2014

Aconteceu no Brasil – Crônicas de um Pesquisador Norte Americano no Brasil II, USA. 2015

It Happened in Brazil – Chronicles of a North American Researcher in Brazil II. USA, 2015

Diário de um Pesquisador Norte-Americano no Brasil III. USA, 2016

Diary of a North American Researcher in Brazil III. USA, 2016

Letters from Brazil. A Cultural-Historical Narrative Made Fiction. USA 2017.

A Professor Takes to the Sea – Learning the Ropes on the National Geographic Explorer.

    Volume I, "Epic South America" 2013 USA, 2018.
    Volume II, 2014 and "Atlantic Odyssey 108" 2016, USA, 2018

Letters from Brazil II – Research, Romance and Dark Days Ahead. USA, 2019.

A Rural Odyssey – Living Can Be Dangerous. USA, 2019.

Letters from Brazil III – From Glad Times to Sad Times. USA, 2019.

A Rural Odyssey II – Abilene – Digging Deeper. USA, 2020

Around Brazil on the "International Adventurer" – A Fictional Panegyric. USA, 2020

Pre – Columbian Mexico – Plans Pitfalls and Perils. USA 2020

Portugal and Spain on the "International Adventurer." USA, 2021

Rural Odyssey III – Dreams Fulfilled and Back to Abilene. USA, 2021

Professor Curran lives in Mesa, Arizona, and spends part of the year in Colorado. He is married to Keah Runshang Curran and they have one daughter Kathleen who lives in Albuquerque, New Mexico, married to teacher Courtney Hinman in 2018. Her documentary film "Greening the Revolution" was presented most recently in the Sonoma Film Festival in California, this after other festivals in Milan, Italy and New York City. Katie was named best female director in the Oaxaca Film Festival in Mexico.

The author's e-mail address is: profmark@asu.edu
His website address is: www.currancordelconnection.com